Pride Publishing books by SJD Peterson:

Love and Rivalry
Essence of the Challenge

I0542056

Love and Rivalry

ESSENCE OF THE CHALLENGE

SJD PETERSON

Essence of the Challenge
ISBN # 978-1-78651-940-5
©Copyright SJD Peterson 2016
Cover Art by Posh Gosh ©Copyright April 2016
Interior text design by Claire Siemaszkiewicz
Pride Publishing

Published in 2016 by Pride Publishing, Newland House, The Point, Weaver Road, Lincoln, LN6 3QN, United Kingdom.

Pride Publishing is an imprint of Totally Entwined Group Limited.

ESSENCE OF THE CHALLENGE

Dedication

For Beccan and Rae, who had to eat a lot of leftovers and takeout while this was being written. Love you both to the moon and back.

"Challenges make you discover things about yourself that you never really knew. They're what make the instrument stretch and what make you go beyond the norm."
~ Author Unknown

Prologue

Dogs may be a man's best friend, but the cute salesman behind the counter in the shoe department at Macy's was Symone's. At least for today. Add in the twenty percent off coupon to her final bill and he was her favorite BFF.

A new happily colored top revived her and the irresistible strappy heels in red were too hard to pass up. It was as if, through shopping, she found a new focus and it lifted her mood. When real life sucked, or was too hard to figure out, retail therapy was the best way to solve it.

Ha! Let's see a dog do all that!

With their mountain of purchases from a very productive morning at the Waterview Mall, Symone followed her best friend, Sedesa, to her little Dodge Neon. After dropping off their packages, they headed to an outdoor café within walking distance.

"I have to admit you were right," Symone acknowledged as she sat at a small bistro table across from Sedesa. "I feel much better. My credit card hates you, but I thank you."

"How long have you known me? You should know by now that I'm always right," Sedesa responded without looking up from her menu.

"Figures you'd keep your head down when you said that. No way could you have done it with a straight face, otherwise."

"Shut up," her friend teased playfully with a flip of her hand. "I'm going to have the Berry Delicious Summer Salad, what about you?"

"Cheeseburger and fries," Symone said without picking up the menu.

"Have I ever told you how much I hate your metabolism?"

"No you don't, you envy it. Besides, I'll eat something light for dinner. I'm starving."

"Skipped the late dinner and went right to dessert, did ya?" Sedesa waggled her brows suggestively.

"No. Travis got tied up in a meeting last night so I skipped dinner in favor of a bag of natural popcorn, mineral water and old *Three's Company* reruns."

Travis, as a new financial advisor with MET Life, couldn't turn down clients. He was still working to build a solid client base and, over the last couple of months, he'd been swamped. Feast or famine, she supposed. She just wished he were home more in the evenings. He'd apologized, but assured her it was for their future.

Instead of whining, she needed to be supportive, but damn it, she missed him. She pushed away the sadness that she'd been wallowing in this morning and that threatened to come back to the surface where it belonged. It was a gorgeous day. She'd spent time with her closest friend and had some sweet new clothes and shoes.

"You should have called me, we could've hung out," Sedesa commented before taking a sip of her water.

"I thought you had a date last night?"

Sedesa wrinkled her nose. "He didn't make it to dessert." She waved off any more on that subject. "People must have money to burn again, invest or whatever. That's, like, what, the fourth time Travis has canceled on dinner this month?"

Fifth, but she wasn't counting or anything.

"He's been really lucky. A lot of the other advisors are struggling, but Travis has a way with people. He's really good at his job." The waitress came and filled their glasses and took their order.

Symone tried not to think about how many dinners he'd missed lately. The weird tightening in her gut was getting annoying and she didn't want to deal with it today. "So how many pairs of shoes does that make now?"

"Forty-two and counting." Sedesa beamed.

Over lunch, Symone kept the conversation away from herself and Travis and focused on Sedesa. Keeping her friend distracted was easy — all she had to do was ask about the men she'd dated, those that had caught her eye or the ones she planned to go out with in the future. If by chance that topic got slow, there was always shoes.

After paying for lunch, Sedesa suggested they check out a new boutique in Clover. Squeezing into the packed Neon, they headed toward Glitz & Glamour Boutique.

Symone was staring out of the window, watching the buildings pass in a blur of colors and shapes when Sedesa screeched. "Damn it!"

Jerking, she turned toward her friend, whose face was bright red, her jaw tight. "God damn it, I hate construction. Are detours really necessary?"

A neon orange *Road Closed* sign flashed its lights, stating the obvious. "Wasn't it you who has been complaining for the last few months that they needed to fix this stretch of road? You got your wish, what's the problem?"

Sedesa huffed, tapping the steering wheel. "The problem is the fucking detour. I hate detours. They never make them clear and I end up getting lost. Hold on," she warned, and gunned the engine, whipping the wheel to the right and turning.

Symone slammed into the passenger door, her arm taking the brunt of it and pain radiating up to her neck. "Christ, Mario Andretti, slow down and give me more of a warning next time." She rubbed the throbbing muscles. "No one gets lost in Wakulla so untwist your panties."

"Sorry, detours are just a pain in the ass," Sedesa apologized and eased off the gas pedal.

They had only made it a couple of blocks when Symone spotted a familiar vehicle parked, partially obscured by an overpass. "Hey, that's Travis' car. Pull over, he must have broken down."

"Are you sure?"

"Yeah, it has the same broken tail light. Just turn there." She pointed to a driveway to turn in to. "Pull around next to it."

Sedesa eased the Neon up beside Travis' car. Part of Symone was shocked by what she was seeing but another part, the logical part, wasn't surprised.

Fate had intervened, sending them on such a detour. Instead of arriving at a cute little shop browsing through aisles of smelly soap and candles, she was sitting in her best friend's car looking at her boyfriend's exposed ass bobbing up and down between spread legs.

In that moment, something shifted deep within Symone. Growing up in a quiet suburb of Detroit, she'd had the fairy tale childhood. Her parents had been devoted not only to their children, but to each other as well. There had been the white picket fence, a soccer mom van in the driveway and ballet classes on Saturday morning. Symone had rarely broken a rule. Not against her parents, teachers or pastors. She'd tried to please everyone. In high school it had been much the same—she'd kept her grades on the honor roll, done community service, participated in after-school activities and sports. She was the all-around good girl.

Sitting there watching Travis' ass as he pounded into some unseen woman, Symone felt numb. He was just another in a series of men who had taken advantage of her wholesome good nature. It had been the same with her first high-school boyfriend, then her college sweetheart and now Travis.

While her goodie-two-shoes ass was crying her eyes out, the naughty women of the world were out having one hell of a good time with the men she was home waiting for. The bad girls didn't wait for men to throw them a few scraps once in a while. They went out and made their own fun.

Sitting in the quiet car—the only sound a low melody playing from the car stereo—Symone watched as Travis threw his head back, his face slack, his lips parted, and felt nothing. She continued to watch as he jerked with the aftershocks of his orgasm, and for a moment, the world stopped when he opened his eyes and his gaze met hers. In that split second, it all became perfectly clear.

A sly smile curled her lips and she winked at the horror-stricken expression on Travis' face, before turning to Sedesa. "Let's go shopping. I saw a pair of stilettos that would be perfect to add to my collection."

Chapter One

The six-month mourning period was over.

Symone wasn't sure it should be called *mourning*, since that would imply there was something sad about the end of her year-long relationship with Travis.

Well, there was the fact that she would miss Lily. The little pug had grown on her, but she wouldn't miss the chewed shoes or the barks at five a.m. that screamed *let me out now*. The loss of Lily sure as hell wasn't enough to want to stay.

She wouldn't miss the 'sorry, I got tied up' excuses, the strange calls from random females on nights she stayed at his apartment and certainly not the 'oh, she's just a client'. Really, because if that's how it worked, her financial advisor was doing it all wrong. Mr. Crompton never once took her out and plied her with drinks at a dance club just to get a look at her portfolio.

Yeah, there wasn't much about Travis' sorry, cheating ass to mourn. She should rename it the grace period. Six months to get her thoughts collected. Six months of being completely selfish, thinking of her own wants and needs and no one else.

Her greatest downfall had always been wearing her heart on her sleeve. Giving her love away without question had gotten her heart shredded more than once. But not anymore. If men could go out on the prowl with only one intention in mind, why couldn't she? Emotions were staying safely tucked away at home tonight. Tonight was for her and her alone. It was her 'coming back to the living' celebration.

Stepping through the door of Menjo's, Symone tried to hide the smirk at the heads that snapped in her direction. She knew she looked good. Damn good.

She had dressed the part of seductress to perfection. Tight black leggings molded her body like a second skin. The silk, midriff-baring top was the perfect match for her eyes. Maybe a tad revealing, but that's what she was going for, wasn't it? At five feet six, one hundred thirty pounds, she was average, but she knew how to work what the good Lord had given her.

The three-inch stilettos just assisted in what he had forgotten to bless her with. She could forgive him for the slight error since he'd given her thick auburn hair that didn't require much beyond a wash and an occasional trim. She wore it free, the tips of it tickling the flesh of her exposed lower back. He'd also graced her with chartreuse green eyes and a clear olive complexion. As more than one man turned in her direction, eyes wide, her average stature and small B-cup size of her breasts seemed all but forgiven.

Making her way toward the back of the club, hips swaying to the beat of the pounding techno music, she caught sight of Sedesa at a small table. She waved and headed toward her.

She ignored the wolf whistles, attempted gropes and invites of nights of pleasure, and took the seat across from her best friend. "Jesus. The dogs are out in full force tonight."

"Woof, woof. You know what they say about the big dogs, don't you?"

"Do you see me sitting on a porch?"

"Oh I wasn't referring to that quote." Sedesa took a sip of her drink, a sly smile on her lips. "I was referring to the one about unleashing the beast, and, honey, that outfit has unleashed a whole club full of beasts."

"This old thing," Symone drawled in her best Violet Bick impersonation. "Why, I only wear it when I don't care how I look."

Sedesa rolled her eyes. She waited until the waitress took their drink orders before continuing. "Honestly, you look amazing tonight. I feel sorry for any chick that sets her sights on the same man you do. Except me of course. You see that blond guy at the end of the bar? He is off limits to you."

Symone turned and looked in the direction Sedesa pointed. Leaning against the end of the bar was a tall, blond-haired mountain of a man. He was dressed in leather pants and a pale blue shirt. He was gorgeous and dressed like he knew it. Though handsome, the way he moved, the cockiness in his stance did nothing to pique Symone's interest.

So not my type. "You have nothing to worry about." Her gaze returned to the dark-haired man standing next to the one who had captured Sedesa's interest.

Oh yes, just my type.

He was tall, his dark hair just long enough that it curled up against the collar of his pale dress shirt. The hint of a dark shadow was prominent on his strong chin and jaw. He wasn't overly muscular but the way he filled out his tight dress slacks and stretched the seams of his shirt, he was definitely built to Symone's exact specifications.

All lean muscle rather than bulk. He had the kind of body that was toned, taut and made for endurance. A tingle raced down her spine as she took in the glorious sight of such perfect man flesh. Warmth spread out across each nerve ending, merging as a sweet ache between her thighs.

The ache intensified as his gaze settled on hers, a slight smile curling the edge of his full lips as he winked. She couldn't look away, enraptured by the sensual current that pulled her toward him.

A slap to her arm snapped her attention back to Sedesa.

"Ow! What the hell was that for?" She rubbed at the sting in her arm.

"I told you to keep your sights off."

"I told you, you don't have to worry about me going for Mr. Cocky. I was checking out Mr. Tall, Dark and Delicious."

"Oops, my bad." Not sounding the least bit sorry, Sedesa turned to study the men. When she turned back, she had a dreamy look in her eyes. "Yeah, he's delish all right. But you know me. I keep hoping to find a big dumb blond that will sweep me off my feet and doesn't mind that I prefer smut over literature."

"Or that you can't cook, don't clean and your monthly shoe allowance is more than most people's mortgage."

Sedesa waved a hand flippantly. "You say that like it's a bad thing."

Telling Sedesa her opinion was interrupted when a drink was set down in front of each of them. "Compliments of the gentleman at the bar."

Symone looked up, praying it was the dark-haired hottie, but the waitress was pointing in the opposite direction. Pouting, she picked up the drink, intending to play an uninterested, but gracious recipient.

When Symone raised her glass in thanks, her breath caught. Sitting with his back toward the bar was another *Oh so my type god*. He was the light to the dark-haired man she'd noticed moments before. His wheat-blond hair was thick, touching the tops of his shoulders. The shape of his face was pure masculine strength beneath golden skin. Strong square jaw, a cleft chin that begged to be kissed, licked and explored. His wide shoulders tapered down from a broad chest to a lean waist. Symone's heart skipped a beat when he raised his glass in response. A shy, sensual smile bloomed across his face, showing perfect white teeth.

"Oh my fucking God, are you not perfection," she mumbled as she raised the glass and gave a slight nod.

Her six months of self-imposed celibacy were making themselves painfully known. Symone tried not to squirm in her seat, but the throbbing ache radiating up from between her legs made it nearly impossible to keep still. She literally vibrated with arousal. She forced herself to look away before she made a complete fool of herself. If she stared any longer, her panting tongue would roll out of her mouth. A drooling puddle of goo was *so* not an attractive first impression.

"Compliments of the gentleman at the other end of the bar," the waitress drawled with barely controlled disgust, as she set a second drink down in front of her on the table.

"Excuse me?"

The waitress pointed toward the bar again. This time she pointed in the direction where the dark-haired man stood. "You're quite the popular girls, aren't you?" She set another drink in front of Sedesa, whirled on her heels and was gone in a streak of bleach-blonde hair and attitude.

Symone ignored Sedesa's giggling and once again looked toward the opposite end of the bar. She met his gaze, his dark brow creased into a deep frown. *Oops*. She picked up the newest glass and raised it in his direction. She gave a small, embarrassed shrug at being caught ogling the blond man and mouthed, "Thank you." She turned away as her cheeks heated.

"Don't even say it." She glared at her best friend.

Sedesa laughed and arranged the drinks that had been set in front of her. "At least they're polite and didn't leave me out. Bat your lashes at a few more dogs and we'll be knee walking without spending a dime."

"Shut up. It's not funny," Symone complained.

"You're right. It's fucking hilarious and I for one am enjoying the shit out of your discomfort," Sedesa snorted.

Symone took a sip of her drink. There was no way in hell she could keep up if the drinks kept coming at this rate, not without making an ass of herself anyway.

"I'm glad you're having so much fun at my expense. Remind me again why the hell you're still my friend?"

"Oh God, I love this song!" Sedesa screamed, ignoring her as she jumped to her feet and grabbed Symone's hand. "C'mon."

She allowed herself to be pulled into the wave of bodies scrambling to the dance floor as Taio Cruz belted out *Dynamite* throughout the club.

Sedesa and Symone sang at the tops of their lungs as they let go and gave in to the music.

The rhythm moved through her. Muscles released hidden tension as she swayed and thrust her hips to the sensual beat. The press of bodies was a heady intoxicant. They danced suggestively against one another. They moved in close, bodies bumping and grinding against each other, spinning away before it became too overheated or X-rated. Giggling into the other's ear as men stopped their gyrations and openly gawked at them. It was a powerful rush, to elicit such lust in others with just the movement of her body.

Though surrounded by willing, glorious male flesh, she found herself searching the crowd for both men who had sent her a drink. As the song changed, she didn't let the disappointment at not encountering either of them ruin the moment.

She loved to dance. She felt alive. The flex and roll of her muscles, the way perspiration trickled down her spine and the lightheadedness sent a rush of arousal across her skin. For the first time in so very long, since first meeting Travis over a year and a half ago, she felt beautiful and desired.

Both she and Sedesa continued to tease and taunt with their bodies. They shook their asses wantonly, thrusting their hips in an effort to make the natives restless. It had obviously been quite successful as when the music morphed into a slower, lovers' tempo, she was inundated with offers to dance. She waved each of them off with a devious smile and a 'maybe next time' as she made her way back to her table.

There was no sense burning any bridges. When she reached the table, a strong hand grabbed hers, stopping her in her tracks. She turned, intending to decline the offer of a dance yet again, but the words died in her throat. She looked up into the deep brown eyes of her dark stranger.

"Can I have this dance?" he asked. His voice was like soft velvet.

Goosebumps erupted from her flesh and a jolt of lust surged throughout her system. With her free hand, she reached for one of the drinks on the table. Without breaking eye contact, she threw back the warm drink, forcing down the lump that had formed in her dry throat. She returned the empty glass to the table, nodded and followed him onto the dance floor.

"I'm Zander," he said as he pulled her into his arms.

"Symone," she replied in a breathless voice.

The heat of his body, the taut muscles rippling and flexing against hers as they began to sway short-circuited her brain. The rich, spicy scent of his skin and rough stubble tickled her cheek as he nuzzled her. Her legs felt as if they wouldn't be able to hold her and she clung to his strength and lost herself in the touch, smell and sight of Zander.

They moved well together. Symone easily followed his lead as they glided across the crowded dance floor. The volume of the music made small talk impossible without screaming, so they let their bodies and hands say hello, nice to meet you. And it was very, very nice to meet Zander. His body was just as hard as it had appeared from across the room.

Thank God! She ran her hand down the sinew of muscle along his back, exhilarated by the way it twitched in response to her touch. From across the room he had been magnificent, but up close, with his spicy musk scent enveloping her, he was glorious.

As the song continued, Symone's long-denied body responded to the press of his. His fingertips at the nape of her neck and the exposed skin of her back sent waves of sensation to dance along her nerve endings. The well-built thigh wedged between hers caused a detonation of desire to burst from her core in jolting contractions and moisture to seep from the walls of her sex.

Zander whispered something indistinguishable close to her ear. Dazed, she nodded and tipped her head farther to the side, giving him plenty of room to work.

I have no idea what you're saying, but if it includes you, me and your lips, I'm all for it.

She loved how the heat and hum of his lips vibrated along her skin.

Symone was easily losing herself in Zander right there on the dance floor. She marveled in the delight of all that was pure male and sweet arousal. All too soon, the song came to an end, changing to a more upbeat tempo, and Symone was snapped from her contentment when a heavy hand landed on her shoulder.

"Mind if I cut in?" The deep baritone voice forced her to pry herself away from Zander and peek over her shoulder.

Standing behind her was the blond Adonis who had also bought her a drink. To say she was a little giddy at the idea of the two most gorgeous men she'd ever seen battling for her attentions was an understatement. It was pure fucking heaven. She didn't know either man and certainly didn't owe either of them anything just because they had bought her a drink. There was also no way in hell she could choose between them.

She shrugged and eased out of Zander's arms. "I have all night. What the hell." A huge smile stretched across her face. She tried hard not to bat her lashes at him, but failed.

He held out his hand and Symone placed hers in his. "I'm Marco."

"I'm Symone and this here is Zander," she yelled over the blaring music and nodded toward Zander. "Pleased to meet you."

Zander and Marco sized each other up. The look on their faces was more a baring of teeth than a smile. The testosterone was so thick in the air that it made her stomach roll. For a moment, Symone held her breath, watching to see how this battle would play out. She half expected the dogs to cock their legs and mark their territory. Intense silence threaded between them. Zander graciously conceded first.

Zander took her free hand in his and placed a small kiss to the back of it. The soft slide of his lips caused her breath to catch. He stood and moved in close to her ear. "He can have the fast beats. The next slow dance is mine." He stepped back, without even acknowledging the way Marco glared at him, but the slightly cocky smile assured her that he hadn't missed it.

Symone couldn't tear her eyes from him as he sauntered across the floor, in the direction of the bar. *Lord have mercy, that is one sweet ass.* She watched in awe at the way his slacks stretched across that perfect ass with each step, until he was out of sight.

She turned her attention back to Marco. "Shall we?"

Marco pulled Symone close to his body, placed one hand in hers and rested the other on her hip.

The moment they began to move, his body responded to hers without conscious thought. It was as if they had always been partners. He tried to keep a respectable distance between their bodies, making a conscious effort not to allow his hands to wander too close to sensitive, private areas. He'd watched her and the dark-haired man dance, surprised to feel unexpected jealousy rise quickly.

He had no idea who she was but from the first moment he'd spotted her across the bar he'd known he had to have her. He had studied his competition. This man, Zander, was good looking, he'd give him that. Marco wasn't too worried, though, he could hold his own in that arena. Somehow, he'd have to tilt that advantage in his direction. Since she had so easily agreed to dance with him after rubbing up close to another man, he would try a different tactic. He would play the role of perfect gentleman.

As they moved to the upbeat tempo, spinning and twirling such a sensual creature as Symone, Marco found that his resolve to be noble was harder and harder to keep.

Each time she came in close, a zing of arousal shot across his nerve endings. Each brush of her hand, however innocent, was like a caress to his growing erection. He spun her, pulled her close and dipped her.

Looking down at her beautiful face and laughing eyes, he was dumbstruck at how gorgeous she was. As if in slow motion, he eased her upright, wrapping his arms tightly around her, his gaze never leaving hers. As he swam in the depths of those stunning green eyes, everything around them disappeared. Their bodies pressed together from head to toe. The sensual glide of her body against his dictated the tempo rather than whatever beat came through the club's speakers.

Marco kept a tight leash on the impulse to grind harder against her. Trying to ignore the way his body screamed to bury itself in Symone's heat, he could barely rein in the desire to feel her lips against his.

Just a taste.

Tentatively, he brushed his lips against hers. She responded, pressing tighter against him. Her hand came up to run through his hair, encouraging him to deepen the kiss. It was all the enticement he needed. He licked at her bottom lip, groaning as he tasted her sweet flavor.

Symone parted her lips and let his seeking tongue inside. He felt overwhelmed by what he could only describe as rightness. He pulled her lean body closer to his as he ravished her mouth. The power in that one kiss left him dizzy and yet it wasn't enough. She gave as good as she got, too, slipping her tongue inside his mouth to taste and explore. His cock was rock hard and threatened to split the seams of his jeans as the kiss went deeper.

The sudden sensation of Symone's body pulling away from his ended their kiss. He snapped his head up, ready to tell off whoever dared to interrupt, only to meet Zander's dark glare and cocky smile.

Bastard.

"Sorry," Zander said curtly. "I do believe this slow dance is mine."

He looked back at Symone, whose eyes were a little glazed, and she was still panting from the kiss they'd shared. He was torn between letting her go to Zander in that state and feeling pretty fucking smug for having put that look there in the first place. He held her gaze for a moment longer, trying to convey through his eyes how much he wanted her, how he hated to let her go.

Reluctantly, he released his grip around her waist.

Let's just see how well you do to top that, hotshot. So that sounded a little pompous but he didn't really give a shit. It was true. He left them after one last kiss to Symone's lips just to piss off Zander and casually walked to the edge of the dance floor. He leaned against a pillar and watched as they moved together.

Enjoy it, buddy. She won't be in your arms for long.

By the time the song had made it halfway through, Marco was fighting the urge to walk back out onto the dance floor and snatch Symone away. He was fighting a crazy fucking caveman mentality. The rational portion of his brain understood why he was still leaning against the pillar watching Zander pull Symone close. That part knew he had no claims to her.

Yet, the rest of him didn't give a shit about being rational. Symone appeared as if she was melting into the dark-haired man, as his hands explored her back, fingers running through her long, dark auburn strands. He should be going after an easier target. There was more than a fair share of drunk and horny women in Menjo's tonight.

Why her? Why *not* her? was the better question. Why go for easy when he could have someone who looked, smelled and moved like Symone?

This is an all-out, balls-to-the-wall situation. May the best man win.

Marco was already moving onto the dance floor before the logical part of his brain caught up to stop him.

Zander stiffened against her at the exact moment a warm, hard body pressed up against her back. She didn't have to turn around to know Marco had joined them on the dance floor.

Good God! It was a stunning sensation to have them both pressed against her. It became all too clear in the blink of an eye...

So why choose?

She tightened the grip she had on Zander's neck and forced him to look at her instead of at the man at her back. With her free hand, she grabbed onto Marco's hip and swayed seductively between the two of them. She held her breath as a tense Zander hesitated. She sighed in relief when he began to move, tentative at first, then matching the slow sway of her hips.

Marco brushed his lips against the side of her throat, sending lust to dance across her nerve endings, heading straight to her core. The spark Marco had ignited burst into pure fire when Zander took her mouth. His tongue darted out to tease its way inside, exploring and arousing. The dual sensation of mouths and bodies was a powerful aphrodisiac that left her trembling.

Zander released her mouth, leaving her moaning as he nuzzled the opposite side of her neck. She settled herself more firmly between their bodies as her knees went weak, letting them hold her up as they assaulted her from both sides with open-mouthed kisses to sensitive flesh. They set the tempo of their slow, passionate dance. The fact that the three of them were moving in perfect rhythm barely registered before she gave herself over to the sensations and simply let the feel of them surround her, rule her mind and body.

If they can do this to me from just a simple kiss and the press of their fully clothed bodies, what would it be like to have their naked flesh pressed against or inside me?

Her trembling increased as the image fully formed in her mind's eye. The thick bulge pressing against her ass pushed her further against the equally hard bulge against her stomach and created the perfect friction. The wet heat between her legs increased with each movement. The walls of her sex contracted as she teetered on the verge of orgasm.

Did they realize how perfect they moved together in their competition? How the movement of one complemented the other? Both men knew exactly when to pull back, when to push. The few ménage stories she'd read in the past were hot as hell but she couldn't help but think that splitting her attention between two men would somehow be distracting. The logistics of numerous arms and legs seemed overwhelming.

Screw logistics. Pleasure is so much better than logic.

She loved being wrong, especially in this case.

As song after song played, each man tried to outdo the other, both working her into a frenzy, keeping her on the verge of orgasm without letting her fall into the bliss she so desperately craved. It was becoming more painful than pleasurable. Her body was being pushed beyond its tolerance and limits.

When she was ready to beg for mercy and sit the next song out, her thighs were cramping and blisters were beginning to form on her toes. She was close to spontaneous human combustion from the amount of raw animal lust being doused over her.

I've seen images of it—nothing left but legs and burnt ashes. She stole a glance at both Zander and Marco. *Hot, but still not worth ending up a pile of ash.*

Back at the table, she had to stifle a laugh. Zander and Marco took a seat on either side of her and each placed a proprietary hand on her thighs. She wondered if they realized how they mirrored each other. Both inched their chairs closer to her and waved a hand at the waitress for service. Marco's heat radiated from her right and Zander's from the left. Now that her brain was surfacing slightly from the lustful haze, it registered how Marco's fresh woodsy scent mingled with Zander's spice and musk, making the perfect combination. Together, even their scents complemented and heightened the others.

"Would you like something to drink?" Marco asked.

She eyed the almost opaque liquid in her glass. "Yes, please." She wrinkled her nose. "My drinks seem to have watered down in my long absence."

"Are you hungry? Would you like me to order you something to eat before the kitchen closes?" Zander queried.

"No, thank you."

"Do you come here often?" Marco quizzed.

I can't believe he'd use that cheesy line. Symone rolled her eyes but didn't answer.

"You're amazing on the dance floor. Are you a professional dancer?" Zander probed.

Okay, that sounded ridiculous. He was trying a little too hard to impress. Still, she smiled graciously. "Thank you, but no, I'm in real estate."

"Do you work close by? What firm are you with?" Marco cut in.

"A small firm out of Wakulla."

"Are you from Tallahassee? Do you live here in the city?" Zander interrogated.

"No, I'm from Michigan originally, and yes, I live here in the city."

They kept firing questions at her in rapid succession, barely giving her time to respond before the next one was asked. As if she could actually concentrate on what they were saying with their fingers dancing along her inner thighs. She was beginning to feel as if she were watching a tennis match. Her head bounced left and right as she responded to whatever they lobbed at her. The muscles in her neck strained from the constant side-to-side movement of her head.

Rubbing at her neck with one hand, she reached for the glass in front of her and took a big gulp. The cool liquid eased her raw throat caused by trying to speak over the loud music. Her shoulders slumped, as more questions were fired at her, her responses coming out broken and incomplete. She shrank into her seat as each question felt like a physical blow. She jerked up as fingers pressed into her inner thighs and began creeping upward.

You're doing it again. You're letting a man, or in this case two men, take control of the moment and the situation. Wake up, girl. She wasn't here to be *picked up*. Her new resolution was one in which she did the choosing. She was the prowler, not the prey.

C'mon, Symone, time to take back a little control. If she didn't, she'd wind up going completely out of her mind and start begging them to ease her ache. She quickly crossed her legs to prevent the seeking hands from moving any higher, before the wet heat radiating from her was discovered.

Dipping her finger into the glass, she pulled an ice cube out and sucked it into her mouth. Both men followed her movements with heated gazes. A wicked idea formed. Using the tip of her tongue, she played with the ice, slowly sucking it in and out of her mouth and letting it melt and overflow from the corners of her lips.

Their questions ceased and they both stared at her with slightly parted lips, their eyes riveted to the ice. Symone sucked it into her mouth, holding it between her teeth as she hollowed her cheeks and sucked forcefully, moaning wantonly. She reached for another sliver of ice from her glass and ran it across her collarbone. She closed her eyes and tilted her head back as she moved the ice up her throat, holding it against her heated flesh, the water droplets running down between her breasts.

Opening her eyes, she stole a glance at both Zander and Marco. They looked at her with heavy lidded eyes. *Gotcha!* "I'm sorry, I was getting a little overheated. Where were we?"

Reinforcements arrived in the form of Sedesa and the blond mountain of a man taking the seats across from her. *Thank God.* It wasn't that she wasn't thankful for Zander's and Marco's attentions, just, damn it, she needed a minute to breathe between questions.

"Hey, Symone, looks like I can't leave you alone for a moment. This is Ian," Sedesa said snuggling up against the big man. She batted her lashes at Marco and Zander. "Who are your two luscious men?" Sedesa openly ogled both of them, a naughty glint mixed with a little jealousy was evident in the twinkle of her eyes.

Introductions were made all around, drinks began arriving and Symone spent the next few hours playing conversation tennis and getting blissfully sloshed to lessen the effects of their simultaneous arousal assault. Thankfully, rum was a hell of a depressant. Still, she wasn't so inebriated that she missed the way Zander and Marco studied each other. It was almost as much as they studied her. They reminded her of two gladiators lying in wait for a weak spot to be revealed. It was both exhilarating and exhausting. By last call, Symone was more than ready to take her drunken ass home, crawl into bed—alone—and pray that the morning hangover wouldn't be too horrible.

Symone downed the rest of her drink in one gulp. *Not like I need it, but at this point it isn't going to make tomorrow morning any better.* Then again, it couldn't make it any worse either. She pulled herself to her feet, thankful for the hands that shot up on either side of her to steady her. "Whew, you two are quite handy to have around, aren't you?"

"Just trying to give a lady a hand," Zander murmured.

"Would you like me to give you a ride home?" Marco inquired.

"If anyone is giving her a ride home it will be me," Zander interrupted as he got to his feet. "How many have you thrown back, Polo?"

"Not as many as you," Marco retorted as he got to his feet, pushing out his impressive chest. "You know, Z, I haven't heard that pet name in a long time. I think the joke stopped being funny to others around the age of ten."

"Want to know what else stopped being funny...?"

Symone took a step back. She wasn't about to be the meat in a beat-down sandwich. "I think I'll just grab a cab. You boys have a good night together." She motioned for Sedesa to follow. "C'mon, we'll share a ride."

The men seemed to come to their senses as Symone grabbed her coat, slung it over her arm and picked up her purse.

"Let me walk you out. Make sure you get to your cab all nice and safe." Marco puffed up a little as he held out his arm, a cocky glint in his eye. He was obviously proud of himself that he'd voiced the idea before Zander had.

"*We'll* walk her out," Zander countered.

She held up her hand to silence them both then dug through her purse in search of her business cards. She might not want either of them taking her home tonight, but she might change her mind in the very near future. It was good to keep her options open.

Finding only one card, she threw it on the table. She pulled a pouting Sedesa away from Ian and waved goodbye. While the boys were distracted in their newest pissing contest, she headed out of the door.

Zander's first thought was to follow Symone, but that would leave the obnoxious dick to snatch up the card Symone had thrown on the table. Just as he shot his hand out to grab it, the blond asshole did the same.

Zander pulled back half a card. *Shit!* "Look, Polo, why don't you give me that and you run along to find someone else to bother? You're out of your league here."

"Really." Marco twirled the other half of the card in his fingers. "Because the way she was rubbing that fine body against mine earlier, it sure didn't feel like I was out of my league. In fact, I think I'll sign up for this team."

Team? There was no *team.* He looked around the diminishing crowd in the club. There were still plenty of women left who hadn't *hooked up* with anyone yet. All he had to do was take his pick. He was sure he could have any one of them in his bed within the next half hour. He looked back at Marco. He didn't need the headache this asshole would surely bring.

Yeah, but you like the thrill of it, don't you?

He thought about that for a moment. The thrill of getting a new partner into his bed had grown old and boring. The opportunity to best Marco for a chance with Symone sounded exciting as hell. Besides, there was something about her. He couldn't put his finger on it, didn't really know her well enough to even try to understand. He just knew he wanted to know her a whole lot better.

Zander looked down at his half of the card. It was solid black with red lettering. Her first name printed above an area code and the first three numbers of a phone number. *Fuck.* No last name, no mention of a company she worked for.

The cocky bastard must have gotten the better half. He searched the crowd but didn't see Symone. She'd been swallowed up by the exiting crowd, and if he didn't come up with some way to pry that little piece of cardboard out of Polo's fingers he might never see her again. Completely unacceptable. The only thing that gave him any sort of comfort was the look on Marco's face when he viewed his half of the card. *Ha! Bastard didn't get any more than I did.*

Marco looked up from the card and met his eyes. "Any chance I can talk you out of your portion?"

Zander pursed his lips. "What do you think?"

"Didn't think so." Marco shrugged. "It was worth a shot, though. Breakfast at the Nugget?"

"You buying?"

"You gonna give me your half if I do?" Marco smirked.

"Nope." Zander slipped his half of the card in the front pocket of his jeans and headed for the front door.

"Then buy your own fucking breakfast," he heard Marco mutter as he fell in step behind him.

The Nugget was the spot everyone headed to when they'd had one too many drinks at Menjo's. It was within walking distance and they served strong coffee and the best pancakes in town. It was exactly what he needed to absorb some of the rye sloshing around in his gut.

Hopefully, while there, he could use his charm to relieve Polo of his half of the card. If all else failed, he could always beat the shit out of the guy in the parking lot on his way out.

After pancakes, of course.

Chapter Two

The vibration of her cell phone against the nightstand brought Symone out of her light sleep. She'd gotten up earlier, popped a few Tylenol for her throbbing head, and downed a huge glass of water into her dry throat. Still feeling like shit, she'd gone back to bed.

The throb in her head had dulled somewhat since she'd woken earlier this morning, but that didn't mean she had any desire to get out of bed any time soon. It was Sunday, for God's sake, a day of rest and all that. More to the point, she didn't feel like answering the phone and listening to Sedesa's overly chipper voice on the other end of the line this early. She was the only one that ever got away with calling on a Sunday morning. Everyone else had learned long ago that the wrath she would rain down was not worth speaking to her before noon. She didn't want to be reminded of how Sedesa never got hangovers, the bitch.

I may be feeling a little better than when I first peeled my eyelids open earlier, but still not well enough for conversation. She pulled the covers over her head and ignored Miss Rosy Fucking Sunshine.

After the third time her cell phone annoyingly sounded, Symone realized that Sedesa wasn't going to give up and she could either lie there listening to the irritating buzz or she could throw it across the room. She groaned, without opening her eyes, and blindly grabbed the phone from the nightstand. Ignoring her initial desire to send it flying across the room, she decided it was cheaper to tell Sedesa to fuck off and power the thing down than have to buy a new one later.

At least I didn't kill all my brain cells with alcohol last night, some of them are still firing. She flipped the phone open.

"Since the gods of hangovers choose to ignore you, I hope the deities of STDs bestow you with rotten crotch," she muttered quietly so as not to aggravate the throbbing in her head.

Before Symone could press the 'Off' button, a deep masculine laugh came through the phone. "I hope you have a Theophoric amulet of protection or, at the very least, know how to appease this deity. I would hate to still be inflicted with rotten crotch at work tomorrow. It sounds very painful and not the least bit pleasant."

"Oh God, I'm so sorry! I thought you were my friend Sedesa. She calls me on Sunday mornings and rubs it in my face about never having hangovers. I have the granddaddy of hangovers. I feel like crap and it's just not fair that..." *Okay, so not very many brain cells are firing properly.* "Sorry, who is this?"

"It really sucks that you're not feeling well. But it just so happens that Grandma's old standby, chicken soup, seems to work as well for hangovers as it does for colds. Interested? I have her recipe."

Now this guy was irritating her as much as an early morning call from Sedesa. What kind of geek knows about ancient Egyptian magic to appease a deity and how to cure a hangover? Not to mention being able to cook old Grandma's homemade chicken soup?

What a tool.

"Look, buddy, no offense, but who the hell are you and what do you want? What the hell part of 'I have a headache and feel like shit' didn't you quite understand?"

"Oh, right. I'm sorry. It's Zander. We met at Menjo's last night."

Symone sat up in bed, instantly smoothing down her crazy bed head, as if he could see her through the line. When someone who looked like Zander knew ancient history and a hangover cure, he was not a geek or a tool. He was fucking perfection.

Yeah, and you just tried to voodoo rotten crotch on the man. Way to go!

"Zander." *The dark hair, gorgeous brown eyes, tight ass smile that had me nearly falling to my knees in worship, Zander? Oh hell yes I remember you.*

"Good morning. Wow, you sound really...awake." This time when the deep chuckle came through the line, it shot through her veins like hot lava heading directly to her center. She knew exactly who was on the other side of the phone line now. Her alcohol befuddled body was instantly on high alert for the chance to feel Zander's body against it.

"I'm not usually a morning person. Let's just say that this morning I had the proper motivation," Zander replied.

"Ah, you won the pissing contest?" So he was gorgeous, smart and fast with his hands. What more could a girl want?

"Excuse me?"

"The pissing contest with Marco. If you're calling me I'm going to assume you snatched up my card."

"Let's just say it was a tie. I got half your card by getting head... I mean by calling head..." Zander huffed out a breath. "Crap! I mean I won a coin toss. But part of the deal was that I call at this ungodly hour."

She couldn't help but laugh at his frustration. The way he sounded when he got flustered was cute as hell. She'd store that information for later use. It was also a point in his favor that he was able to compromise and keep his end of a deal. "Part of the deal, huh?"

"Uh yeah, that assho...I mean Polo got one half of the card. I got the other. Look, I only have until noon to get you to have lunch with me. Polo will be calling you then and if I can't... Never mind, would you like to have lunch with me?"

Symone sat up even straighter. Now this was interesting as hell, two top dogs competing over her. More than interesting, it was flattering as hell, exciting.

Oh, who in the hell was she kidding? It was fucking mind-blowing. *Travis, wherever you are, thank you for being a cheating dickhead.*

If he hadn't cheated and been an asshole, she wouldn't be sitting here with a dark sexy god asking her out and a blond one planning to call her later. She would have to send Travis a thank-you note, perhaps even a bouquet of flowers. Hell, if this worked out as well as she hoped, she'd send him a box of goddamn Godiva chocolates.

"I'd love to have lunch with you, Zander."

"Any chance I can have you out of the house by noon?" he asked quietly.

"Now, now, play nice," Symone chuckled. "It's a cell phone. It won't matter if I'm home or not."

"Can't blame a guy for trying. I was thinking we could have lunch at Posey's. Are you familiar with it?"

That scored him bonus points. She loved Posey's. It was located on the pier and was one of her favorite places to dine. Their outdoor dining area extended out past the shoreline and the view was a spectacular complement to their amazing food and service.

She smiled. "Yeah, I'm familiar with it,"

"Great, if you give me your address, I—"

"Ah, ah, ah, not going to happen," she interrupted. "No offense but how do I know you're not some psycho creep?"

"Oh, and she's smart too," Zander teased. "Fine, deprive me of showing off my driving skills. I'll have to come up with another way to impress you."

With the way Zander looked, he could impress her by just sitting there and not laughing when she started to drool. "I'm sure you'll come up with something."

"I'll do my best. Shall we say noon at Posey's then?" he asked.

"Perfect. I'll see you then."

"And, Symone?"

"Yes?"

"I'll have my phone for emergencies, no need to have two."

"Nice try. Bye, Zander." Laughing, she set the phone on the nightstand and headed for a shower.

The warmth of the water washed away the last of the effects of her overindulgence in rum. She was normally the type to stand under the spray until the water turned cold, but this morning she felt like a kid getting ready for a trip to Disney World. She made quick work of her shower and, after drying off, dressed in a simple sundress of white gauze. The back plummeted low, showing off her tan, and the fabric clung to and accentuated her curvy ass. The dress was nearly sheer through the bodice area but there was still enough coverage to conceal areas that would get her arrested for indecent exposure. It was risky, feminine, and she loved every inch of it. She completed her ensemble with wedge heels, ignoring the ache from last night's blisters.

It hurts to be beautiful, she reminded herself, but the way the heels showed off her shapely legs made enduring the pain much more tolerable. Normally she wouldn't wear something quite so revealing on a first date, but she felt empowered. Besides, she needed something to even the playing field with Zander. If she was going to sit across a table from him in one big pile of lust-hazed goop, then it was only fair that he was too. Tit-for-tat, as they say.

Symone applied a little light makeup and ran a brush through her hair. Staring at her reflection, she had to admit she didn't look half bad. A little Visine to clear up her red, dry eyes, and some Preparation-H cream to take down the puffiness around said eyes — *hemorrhoids are not the only thing this stuff shrinks* — and voilà, hidden hangover.

When her cell phone buzzed, she glanced at the display — twelve o'clock on the dot. Marco was punctual, which scored him a couple of brownie points. She couldn't help but grin like a fool as she picked up the phone and flipped it open. "You should have picked heads."

"That will teach me to have that extra Jack and Coke. My reflexes were a little sluggish."

Jesus, she remembered just what a powerful weapon that deep baritone voice was. Her heart literally skipped a beat and she felt lightheaded. Desire ignited to a three-alarm fire in a blink of an eye. Symone grabbed the edge of the sink to steady herself as a shudder ripped through her entire body.

Okay, you're going to have to learn a little control if you plan on running with the big dogs. She wasn't sure how she was going to manage that when just the sound of his voice had her brain taking a vacation.

"I gather the zoo keeper told you about the little incident with the card?" Though he tried to hide it with a small chuckle, she didn't miss the irritation in his voice.

"Oh, you mean Zander?" she replied with syrupy sweetness. She winked at her reflection in the mirror. "He coaxed me out of bed this morning, told me all about the little mishap the two of you had with my card." She bit down on her lip to keep from laughing aloud at the dead silence on the other end of the line. Zander hadn't actually said very much about it, but no sense letting Marco know she was at a disadvantage. "He did say you would be calling."

"Did he now? And did he ask you out to lunch?"

"Uh-huh, we're meeting at Posey's on the pier. Wasn't that sweet of him?" She was being a little evil. In her defense, these two had worked out some kind of compromise so she needed to do a little catching up in this game.

"Oh yeah, real sweet of him," Marco replied sarcastically. Were those molars she heard grinding?

"Then again, seeing as the two of you worked this out beforehand, you knew he was going to be asking me out for lunch. So I'm sure your call wasn't to inquire about my lunch plans."

"Actually, I was hoping you'd turned him down. Any chance I can convince you to change your mind?" Marco asked wryly.

Symone's grin grew wide. "Now why would I do that? I love Posey's."

"If you're going because of the food then I still have a shot." He chuckled. "Hey, would you mind if I called you later? I'd love to hear all about your lunch and maybe even set up some plans of our own? Say five o'clock?"

"Absolutely, talk to you soon."

"Until then."

She ended the call with the sneaky suspicion that she'd be talking to Marco a lot sooner than five o'clock considering she'd let it *slip* where she would be. *Shame on me.*

She smiled as she turned off the bathroom light and headed out. This was so worth being pulled out of bed early on a Sunday morning.

Not one, but two gorgeous men were chasing her. Twice the chance of having not only a good day, but a great one.

I love these odds. Yay me!

* * * *

Symone was reminded of why she loved Florida the moment she stepped out of the car in the parking lot of Posey's. The sound of the gulf in the distance was like music and the smell of sunshine mixed perfectly with the slight salty air. The temperature was in the mid-eighties and the humidity was low for a change. The afternoon was absolutely perfect.

She'd been living in Florida ever since graduating from Central Michigan University two years before. She'd had grand plans of moving to Florida's capital city with her degree in political science in hand and making her mark. Sure, she could have chosen somewhere else, but, after the first twenty-two years of her life being in a state where winter lasted longer than summer, she had set her sights on warmth. What she had got was a decent job in real estate without needing the degree she'd struggled so hard to get. But she was warm at least.

"Hi. Welcome to Posey's." The hostess greeted her with a warm smile as she stepped into the restaurant. "Will you be dining alone this afternoon or will someone be joining you?"

The amazing smells of grilled fish, rich butter and a multitude of spices wafting out from the kitchen filled Symone's nose, and her stomach growled in response. She walked to the hostess stand and returned the smile. "Actually, I'm meeting someone." She looked around the restaurant but didn't see Zander among the other diners. "I'm Symone Adams. I'm meeting a gentleman by the name of Zander."

The smile on the hostess's face fell as she looked Symone up and down with an appraising glance. "If you'll follow me."

Guess Zander is here after all. She followed the newly frozen ice princess toward the back and purposely stopped while she waited for her to open the door that led out to the deck. She was used to women treating her with barely masked hatred, something that never ceased to amaze her. Although she tried not to let it bother her, the truth was it still stung each and every time. They knew nothing about her, yet they assumed that because of her looks she was somehow untouchable and without feelings.

In high school, Sedesa had been her only friend and had stood beside her even when rumors about her had flourished. The worst of which were the ones that she was a bitch and a slut. If anyone had just taken the time to talk to her, they would have found out that not only was she a virgin, but she also had very few friends. She knew she was above average in looks and she wasn't so stupid as not to realize the effect she had on men. She'd known that once she'd first hit puberty, but she'd never imagined it would be such a liability either. It wasn't like she was high maintenance or anything even remotely close to it. Her makeup consisted of mascara, lip gloss and the occasional concealer. Surprising to some, but nonetheless true, because, 'yes Virginia', there are skin blemishes there.

She didn't spend time in the beauty shop, didn't use fancy hair products, or curling or flattening apparatuses. The one time she'd mentioned to a classmate that she didn't spend a lot of time in front of the mirror, she'd gotten an eye-roll and a cold shoulder. She was damned if she did and damned if she didn't.

This was a first for her, a female giving her the cold shoulder for who she was meeting rather than her looks. And, to be honest, it felt a whole lot better. In fact, she couldn't help but preen a little.

As she stepped out onto the deck and spotted Zander rising from his chair, she suddenly wished she'd done a whole lot of primping in the mirror. He was dressed in tan, lightweight linen slacks that accentuated his lean hips and muscular thighs. The white knit pullover was stretched taut across his chest, displaying the hard muscles beneath. Sweet arousal coursed through her body at the very sight of him, sending tingles and jolts to the most delicious places. Heaven help her, he was hot.

She willed her wobbly legs to carry her to him. The ten feet between them felt like ten miles and anticipation grew with each step. At the table, she took his offered hand. As soon as their flesh made contact, the licks of a flame sprang to life. As he leaned in and placed a soft kiss against her cheek, the flame ignited into bright and colorful fireworks. Although she tried, she wasn't able to hide the gasp that emanated from deep within her.

"You look amazing," Zander purred against her cheek before he leaned back. He released her hand and stood behind her chair as he waited for her to sit. Once seated, he gave her chair a gentle push toward the table and returned to his chair.

The man actually purred, like a large predatory cat. It left Symone dazed and was beyond sexy. Zander had that same look in his eyes she'd seen numerous times when men looked at her. The one that said 'I want to rip your clothes off, have my wicked way with you and make you scream'.

For the first time in her life, as she looked into those smoldering brown eyes, she didn't try to look for anything more than the physical attraction. Maybe it was the fact that she was finally growing up, leaving fairy tales and Prince Charming behind. Perhaps it had a lot to do with the harsh realities of life that Travis had taught her, but, whatever it was, she was sure her eyes reflected the same feral look that Zander currently had swirling through his. The idea of taking what she wanted from this gorgeous creature was potent. She understood that it was a purely physical reaction that was void of any emotional conjecture, and at the moment she could live with that.

"Thank you for inviting me." She was not quite as calm as she sounded.

Zander took her hand and stroked her palm. "The pleasure is all mine. What would you like to drink?" Before she could answer, he added, "They have an amazing house wine, a delicious red Cabernet blend. If you're looking for something a little stronger, I'd suggest sex on the beach." His grin was sly.

Symone held his gaze and fought the urge to squirm in her seat. "I'm impressed you were able to say that with a straight face." *Hell, I'm impressed I'm not jumping to my feet and leading you a few yards below to said beach.* "Water with lemon is fine," she said around the lump that suddenly formed in her throat.

Zander shrugged. He tried for innocence with a slight smile, but wasn't quite able to pull it off. The look in his eyes gave him away. He couldn't hide the fact that he'd only been partially kidding.

"Hey, Z, your usual or would you like a menu?" The waiter gave Symone an appreciative once-over and handed her a menu.

"You know what I like, Cam." He gave Symone's hand a slight squeeze. "But give the lady a few moments. In the meantime, she'll have a glass of iced water with lemon and I'll take some more tea please."

The warmth from Zander's hand spread up her arm and the only thing she could think of was how that warm hand would feel caressing her body. Her heart rate sped up. "Actually I'm ready. I think I'll have your fried seafood sampler with extra sauce please." She handed Cam back the menu.

"Finger foods. Yum!" Cam took the menu and gave Zander a wink. "Two Posey Platters coming up."

"I take it you've been here before?" Zander asked.

"Once or twice." She tilted her head and studied Zander. She really knew nothing about the man across from her. He and Marco had fired off questions so rapidly last night that neither of them had really given her a chance to learn anything about them.

"The food is excellent and most of the staff knows me, so I tend to come here a lot. It's like going home for a meal except I don't have to help with the dishes."

"My turn for twenty questions. Where is home?"

"That's fair," Zander agreed as Cam placed their drinks on the table. "Thanks, Cam." He took a long drink from his tea and waited for Cam to move away before answering. "I'm from Louisiana originally. A small town called Hackberry, but I've been here in Tallahassee since I was about twelve."

Symone took a sip of water. The dryness in her throat was from more than just the Florida heat. The way Zander spoke, looked at her and how he continued to hold her hand while his fingertips drew designs against her palm had a whole lot more to do with it. It was also the reason for the ache that was settling between her thighs and the catch in her breath as she tried to speak.

"So I'm curious about this little incident between you and Marco last night. You never did tell me exactly what it was you were flipping a coin for."

Zander leaned back in his chair, keeping hold of Symone's hand. He settled into his chair and entwined their fingers. "Let's just say we found it necessary to compromise. I got lucky and won the flip of the coin. I got to have lunch with the most beautiful woman I have ever seen. And Polo…" The lopsided grin on Zander's face turned into a sly leer. "Let's just say it wasn't his lucky night."

Symone blushed at the compliment and tried not to duck her head. It was hard to hold his gaze and not give away the battle that was raging through her. The sexual tension that began to whirl around them was intoxicating. Her body begged to give in to the naughty visions that were flashing through her mind and make them a reality.

Luckily, her brain hadn't taken a complete vacation. She was sure that crawling across the table in a busy restaurant and ripping Zander's clothes off would not be appropriate in a public dining area. Inappropriate or not, the image of Zander sprawled out, those hard muscles beneath her, had her vibrating in her seat as the sweet ache between her thighs grew to a painful need.

Okay, Symone, deep breath. How's that six month grace period working for you now?

Groaning, she forced her gaze away from Zander and fidgeted with the straw in her glass. She could still feel his gaze boring into her and forced herself to sit still.

"Everything okay?" Zander inquired, his voice teasing.

Her cheeks heated further. She might know what she wanted and had a good idea how to go about getting it, but it was still new territory. The seductress, the one to be the aggressor, was foreign to her. Somehow, she was going to have to get used to it — or need iron pills from the constant blushing. She sighed in relief for the distraction when Cam returned to the table. He placed their order in front of them. After refreshing their glasses and making sure they didn't need anything else, he left them to enjoy their lunch.

Symone dipped a scallop in cocktail sauce then popped it into her mouth, sucking the sauce from her fingers. She looked up to catch Zander staring at her mouth as she licked the last of the sauce from her fingertips. Feeling a little wicked—no sense in her being the only one with naughty thoughts—she picked up a fried shrimp, dipped it into a cream butter sauce and brought it to her lips. She licked a drip of butter and playfully ran her tongue along the shrimp before she ate it.

Zander's eyes darkened as he watched her, his breathing increased. He pulled his hand from hers and placed his warm palm on her thigh as he continued to watch her eat. The pressure of his hand on her leg was inviting. She reached for her water glass and took a few sips, trying to get herself back under control before she gave in to the tantalizing invitation.

Over lunch, Symone continued to tease Zander with her sensual meal. In between bites, she learned that Zander had one brother, or was it a sister? He mentioned something to do with his parents and Arizona. He was twenty-seven, had no kids and had never been married. She had paid attention to that part. The rest of it had been difficult to concentrate on. The way his lust-filled gaze never strayed from her mouth as she ate. The way his strong fingers would tighten on her thigh every time she licked her lips. She might be the one trying to tease, but that didn't mean she wasn't feeling the effects.

No, it's backfiring and you need to get control of yourself.

Meg Ryan's famous scene in *When Harry Met Sally* could be mild compared to what she'd started in this restaurant. It was becoming increasingly busy and there was a growing number of families with children arriving. The patio area became crowded with the mild temperatures of the day, so it was time to pay more attention to the conversation and less to the seduction tactics.

"What is it you do for a living?" she asked as she took a bite of her Kahlua and cream cheesecake. She looked up to see Zander watching her mouth again as she savored the flavor. His hand moved up higher on her thigh. Her insides clenched at the tantalizing brush of thick fingers against her sensitive skin.

His gaze zeroed in on her mouth as she swallowed a bite. Zander cleared his throat and met her eyes. "I guess you could say I'm a financial advisor."

Symone was thankful she'd already swallowed the last bite or she would have choked on it.

Wait, what do I care if he has the same job as Travis? It's not like I plan on marrying him. "That's interesting."

"You went a little pale there. You have something against financial advisors?"

She took another bite of her dessert and shrugged. "Not really. You just don't seem the type."

"Ah, no pocket protector?" he teased. "Actually I use the term loosely. I created a computer program that basically makes finance a little easier for large corporations to manage."

"Wow, I'm impressed."

"It's not really all that impressive, trust me. I spent a lot of years traveling from one state to the next, living in one hotel or another. Fortunately, I have a few people to do the traveling for me. Now, I only travel for major contracts or" —he shrugged, a sly smile curling his lips— "pleasure."

She licked the last of the cheesecake from her fork playfully and met his heated gaze. "And do you indulge in pleasure often?" So much for trying to keep her mind out of the gutter, but, hell, the man was built for wicked delights.

Zander leaned in and murmured seductively into her ear, "You're a very naughty little minx, aren't you?"

Symone shifted in her seat. Her mouth was suddenly dry again and her heart pounded with excitement. The erotic images that had been running through her head since she'd first sat down were on a continuous loop. In her mind's eye, she'd already envisioned him in every conceivable position and imagined what every inch of his luscious skin would feel like against her lips. The warmth of his lips against the sensitive flesh below her ear as he spoke sent her nearly tumbling over the edge. "You don't know the half of it," she said breathlessly as she tilted her head back, giving him more room to work.

"I want to know all of it," he whispered against her skin between soft kisses.

She moaned softly as her stomach did a flip-flop. "Yes," was all she could manage under the onslaught of Zander's mouth.

A throat clearing and a small chuckle made Symone snap back from Zander. The heat that had been converging between her legs suddenly made a mad dash for her checks as Cam gave her a wry smile.

"Is there anything else I can get the two of you?"

"Just the check." Zander spoke to Cam but his gaze never left hers. The fingers of the hand resting on her thigh began stroking in a slow rhythm, inching closer to the edge of her moist panties.

Symone used the last of her control to stop from pressing hard into that teasing hand. She swallowed a moan before it could escape her lips with great effort. The smile on his handsome face grew. He knew exactly what he was doing to her. *Bastard.*

"It's not as romantic as it would be in the moonlight, but I'll do my best if you'd like to walk the beach in the sunshine with me?" Zander offered.

"I'll be sure to hold you to that."

Romance wasn't really what she was looking for. Words like 'raw', 'animalistic', 'carnal' and 'mind-blowing' would better describe what she wanted but she'd take romance for now. Amazing how betrayal and a lack of sex could suddenly change her so drastically. It had always been romance before sex—now she couldn't give a shit about romance. *Bring on the pleasure.*

Zander stood and offered her a hand. She took it and stood on shaky legs. Zander dropped money onto the table then led them to the stairs that descended to the beach. Symone said a little prayer in hopes that the beach would be deserted.

At the moment, she wanted nothing more than to be alone with him and show him just what a naughty little minx she could be.

Chapter Three

The warm breeze and ocean spray coming off the gulf caused the sheer fabric of Symone's dress to cling to her body. Zander wasn't sure which was the more powerful — the fact that her body was a work of perfection, the way she carried herself or the look in her incredibly green eyes that shot a jolt straight to his groin. Together they were like a sucker punch to his spiraling-out-of-control libido.

As they walked along the edge of the beach, there was no doubt Zander wanted to ravish the stunning beauty at his side. Wanted to bury himself deep inside her and take his pleasure. His aching shaft attested to how badly he wanted her. It was hard to concentrate beyond the constant throb, but there was something about her that a quick suck and fuck couldn't cure.

His usual need for uncomplicated pleasure just didn't seem like it would be enough when it came to Symone. He loved the fire in her eyes. Her playfulness over lunch had been exciting but he'd also gotten a peek at the real Symone at times. The way she blushed so easily at just a simple compliment. There had also been that look in her eye when he'd first told her he was a financial advisor — he had gotten a glimpse of raw pain, before she'd covered it up quickly. She was complicated. More importantly, her complexities were fascinating as hell and he wanted nothing more than to explore every one of them.

"This right here is why I don't miss Michigan." Symone released his hand and spun in the foamy waves at the edge of shore, arms outstretched, head tilted back as she raised her face to the sun. Jesus, had he ever seen anything so beautiful? His chest squeezed around his heart at the simple joy he was witnessing.

Zander moved closer, grabbed onto Symone's waist and pulled her hard against his body. He sought out the exposed flesh of her back with his hands. Leaning down, he whispered against her neck, "This is why I would never live anywhere else." He placed a soft kiss against her sun-warmed flesh. "I love the taste of sunshine."

Symone's arms came up and wrapped around his neck, drawing him even closer. He hissed as her body pressed harder against his engorged cock.

"What does sunshine taste like?" she asked, a seductive lilt to her voice.

For a moment, he couldn't speak. His body reveled in the feel of her against him, waves of lust rolling off him as powerful as the pounding surf at his feet. He nuzzled her neck, let his tongue snake out and lick the salt from her skin.

He groaned at the flavor. "It tastes like heat, passion," he said, his lips and tongue accentuating every word. "Sparks against my tongue." He moved up her neck, across her jaw until his lips were against hers. "Tempting." He traced her bottom lip with the tip of his tongue. "Mouthwatering."

Symone's lips parted on a moan, and Zander plunged into the sweet, wet warmth of her mouth. She ran a hand through his hair, fisted it, and returned the kiss with a fierceness that rivaled his own. She didn't hold back and let him control the kiss, her tongue battled against his in a fight for dominance. He dropped one hand to the curve of her ass and forced her closer still. He didn't try to hide his arousal—instead he pressed his cock harder against her stomach. He wanted her to know exactly what effect she was having on him, how badly he wanted her.

As the kiss deepened, became increasingly more intense, Zander was forced to lift his head and gasp for air. "Jesus."

Symone panted past red, swollen lips as her intense green eyes bored into his. Still fisting his hair in a tight grip, she nodded.

Zander couldn't think of anything he would rather do than spend the afternoon exploring her sweet mouth. Well, other than spending the afternoon exploring her mouth and every inch of her body, but the peal of laughter from somewhere to his left reminded him they weren't alone. "What I wouldn't give for a deserted beach right now."

Symone laughed and released her grip on his hair. "My reputation saved by the sun worshipers."

Sighing out of frustration, he placed one last kiss to her lips then reluctantly released her. He took her hand and steered them back toward Posey's. Not an easy task considering the way his pants had tented and the deep ache in his balls made walking a little difficult, as well as slightly painful.

As they reached the top of the stairs to the deck of Posey's, Zander stopped and his wish for a deserted beach was even greater.

Sitting at the table he and Symone had occupied earlier, was Marco. He had a sly smile on his face as he tapped a finger against his watch.

Fucker. Why the hell did I ever agree to this?

Unfortunately, he was always a man of his word. Normally, it was a noble trait that he liked owning, but today he hated it.

Zander had stopped on the last stair, his body rigid.

Symone peeked around his broad shoulders, scanned the area until her eyes came to rest on Marco. She'd had the sneaky suspicion he was going to show up after their phone call earlier but hadn't realized how much she'd wanted to see him again until this moment.

The sight of him brought her back to reality. Zander had been true to his word, the stroll on the beach had been as romantic as any midnight stroll. She had lost herself so completely in his kiss.

I can't afford to be lost.

Marco being there was a reminder to brush her feelings off her sleeve and tuck them safely away. She'd promised herself that she was going to think of only herself, as hard as that was to do—she was determined to keep any kind of emotional ties out of the equation.

Sex is not love. Sex is an unemotional pleasure, exciting, and a physical need I want sated. She repeated the mantra until she began to believe it and returned her attention to Marco.

He sat at their table, his legs crossed, leaning back in a casual position as he tapped a finger against his watch. The smile on his face was breathtaking.

Wiggling past Zander, she headed toward Marco with a reluctant Zander in tow. "Well, well, fancy meeting you here," she said with fake shock.

She might not have known for sure whether he would show up, but some part of her had hoped for it. After all, she had told him where they would be having lunch. That little tip she'd passed onto him hadn't had anything to do with an advertisement for the place.

Marco's smile went from sly to dazzling as he stood and reached out a hand toward her.

"More like freakish," Zander muttered.

She ignored Zander's comment, dropped his hand and took Marco's. He pulled her into a tight embrace. "I couldn't wait to see you again," he spoke against her neck, but loudly enough for Zander to hear. They were still playing the pissing game and that was fine with her. Seeing that she was the prize they were competing for, she figured no matter the outcome, it was a win-win situation for her.

Marco lifted his head and spoke to Zander, "It's five o'clock—don't you have some place to be?"

Symone pulled away from Marco's embrace. "Now don't be rude. Zander and I were having a lovely afternoon," she chastised lightly.

She had to bite down on the inside of her cheek to keep from laughing when she turned and saw the scowl on Zander's face. It was quite adorable really. She took a seat at the table and grabbed Marco's water glass. The raw, male testosterone that was swirling through the air was a thick, nearly tangible thing that teased at her skin.

The heat of the afternoon suddenly seemed to pale in comparison to the heat racing through her body, and her throat went dry. Taking a couple of sips of the water, she stole a glance over the rim of the glass at the two men still squaring off. Neither man said anything, but if looks could kill, she'd have a couple of corpses at her feet.

"Gentlemen, shall we have a drink?" She waved a hand indicating the empty seats on either side of her. "Since I seem to be at the center of your little arrangement, perhaps you'd like to bring me up to speed?"

They glared at each other for a moment longer, then took seats at her side. It was déjà vu. Just as the night before, they pushed their chairs closer to hers and each placed a proprietary hand on her thighs, as they inched closer. Symone couldn't help the small gasp that their closeness provoked, nor did she have any control over the contractions rippling through her core. They were sexy as hell. How could they not affect her?

Marco broke the silence first. "Zoo-man here had until five to sweep you off your feet." He squeezed her thigh. "Since he obviously failed and you're still standing, now it's my turn to show you how it's done properly."

"The name is Zander, or is that too difficult for your wee brain to handle? Shall I spell it out for you? Maybe that would help?" Zander huffed.

Marco cocked his head and studied Zander for a moment. "Should I be concerned that you're thinking about my wee brain? The larger of my two brains is screaming, I like it!"

Zander's mouth gaped and his eyes widened, before getting himself back under control. "Fuck off, Polo."

Marco chuckled at Zander's obvious discomfort. "Now who's having difficulties?"

Symone interrupted Marco with a jab of her finger to his chest. "Hush, you." She turned and met Zander's eyes. "Did you agree with this arrangement?"

Zander held her gaze a moment. She watched as a battle played out in his eyes. He thought about stubbornly denying it before he finally resigned himself to the truth and gave a quick nod. "But that was before I actually had time to spend alone with you." He reached up with his free hand and rubbed his thumb gently across her bottom lip. "Now I don't want to share."

Normally Symone was very sensitive when it came to others' feelings. She should have felt guilty about looking forward to spending time with Marco, or at least have felt bad that Zander wasn't happy about it. On some level, she did. She pushed it down, instead concentrating on the tingling sensation Zander's caress produced. The word *share* from his mouth brought to mind images of two sexy men, gloriously naked and herself sandwiched between them.

As the image evolved, the tingle moved down her body and blossomed lower. Zander might not want to share her, but her body sure as hell wanted him to share. The increased moisture between her legs and the now steady ache was proof of how badly her body craved just that.

Jesus, you sound like a wanton hussy.

She told the little prudish voice in her head to shut the hell up. What had being a good girl gotten her? A cheating dickhead for a boyfriend who had spent his evenings having the time of his life while she'd sat at home planning her TV line-up for the night or curled up with a good book instead of a warm body.

Screw that!

She didn't need a reminder of why her heart was strictly off limits. Nor had she forgotten just how wonderful Travis had been before he'd suckered her into believing he loved her. Lies. *Everything he told me was lies.*

Shaking her head to dispel the unwanted thoughts, she focused on the here and now. On the two gorgeous men on either side of her and the weight of their hands against her thighs. No bad memories were allowed here. Her body responded in a pleasurable wave of warmth. The word *share* took on a whole new meaning. Her new motto would be 'the more, the merrier'.

Symone captured Zander's thumb in her mouth, slowly pulling back, then let her teeth rake lightly across the surface as she released it. "Didn't your mama teach you it's nice to share sometimes?" A spark raced down her spine when Zander swallowed hard and licked his dry lips.

His lustful gaze was like a physical touch. "I learned to share just fine." The fingers on her thigh tightened, and Zander's voice dropped to a husky whisper. "But I always had one special thing that I didn't have to share."

Heart pounding in her chest, Symone held his gaze for a moment then turned to Marco. "What about you? Did you learn to share just fine or are you a greedy boy?"

The heavy hand on her other thigh inched higher. "I'm a very greedy boy," Marco whispered seductively. "But I've been known to share." He kissed the sensitive flesh below her ear. "If properly motivated."

The clearing of someone's throat had Symone jumping back in her seat. She felt a flush of heat race up her neck to her checks when she looked up at a smiling Cam.

You have got to be kidding me. Caught twice in the span of a few hours.

She wasn't sure which was going to do her in first — the lust or embarrassment. Never had blood rushed up and down so quickly. One minute it was rushing south, the next, displaying it's self prominently on her cheeks.

"Will you all be dining with us tonight?" Now Cam's chuckle was pure mischief.

This was getting ridiculous. She might be entertaining ideas of being very naughty, but that didn't mean she wanted the world to know. Her first thought was to order a very stiff drink to help with her courage then she thought better of it. Her stomach was just now starting to recover from the night before, no sense torturing it further. She shook her head. "I'm not hungry. I'll just have a glass of water with lemon, please."

"I'll have another glass of wine." Marco glared at Zander. "Z-Man here was just leaving."

Zander returned Marco's glare, with an equally insolent look, before finally saying. "Yeah, I was just leaving. Thanks anyway, Cam."

Once a laughing Cam moved out of earshot, Zander stood and pulled Symone to her feet. "I had a great time today. Can I call you later?" he asked as he hugged her to him.

"So did I. I'd like that," she said sincerely.

"If she isn't too busy," Marco muttered.

They both ignored him, as Zander's lips pressed against hers. The kiss was soft, a tease of something scrumptious, that left her craving more as he eased back and looked down at her. "Until then."

Symone could only nod, her voice stolen by the rush of excitement that Zander ignited in her. As she watched him confidently stroll toward the exit, she wanted nothing more than to call him back, to suggest that they all get cozy and get to know each other in the physical sense. But the two of them had made this agreement and were sticking to it — she'd try to do the same.

Besides, Zander had had his time alone with her and she had been more than a little impressed with his effort. It was Marco's turn for his shot at alone time. She smiled to herself.

Fair is fair, there is always next time.

Once Zander had disappeared from sight, she lowered herself back into her chair, afraid her weak knees would no longer hold her weight. Turning to Marco, she took a deep breath and said, "What was that about being too busy?"

Chapter Four

Marco had watched as Zander had stood and pulled Symone to her feet, wrapping her in a hug. The surge of jealousy that had ripped through him shocked the hell out of him, just as irrational as it had been the night before, but there it was. He wasn't a jealous person, ever, then again he'd never been in this situation either.

He'd always loved the thrill of setting his sights on someone he found desirable and the challenge of getting them into his bed. Most of the time, it really wasn't that much of a challenge, there seemed to always be a willing female to share his bed with.

Zander had added a new element to the game and Marco could appreciate what Symone saw in him. The man was good looking, and as much as he hated to admit it, he could see the appeal of his brooding dark looks. Where Marco was built thick with muscle, Zander was lean, yet still gave the impression of power.

His body had tightened at the first stirring of attraction to Zander, but he'd pushed it down quickly, ignoring the sudden spark. He'd focused on Symone as she'd returned to the seat next to him, all thoughts of Zander beginning to wane as he admired the swell of her pert breasts, small waist and luscious hips. He knew the addictive taste of her skin, and could imagine what those thick chestnut waves would feel like against his body. Her full pouty mouth was made for all kinds of wicked pleasures, and the mischief in those green eyes said she was more than capable of delivering.

Oh hell yeah, Symone was worth having to deal with the arrogant bastard Zander. The pulse of attraction Zander stirred in him was an added bonus.

The way Symone's skin had flushed when Zander had kissed her, and the way her eyes followed him as he'd walked away, meant that he knew he had some catching up to do. "So tell me," he drawled as he draped his arm over the back of her chair. "What would you like to do this evening? Preferably something that will make you forget all about your lunch date."

"That would have to be something pretty damn impressive." Symone laughed softly. "It was quite the lunch."

He leaned in closer and whispered, "Is that a challenge?"

Symone tilted her head to the side and studied him, a playful smile tugging at her lips. "Yes, I believe that is exactly what it is."

He reached out and ran the tip of his index finger along the soft skin of her cheek, his shaft hardening further in response to the shudder his touch elicited from her. "I accept," he said before placing a soft kiss to her lips.

Standing, he pulled his cell phone from the clip on his belt. "I'll be right back," he told her as he moved away from the table.

Symone watched Marco walk to the far side of the deck as he talked on the phone. Good God, what a sight he was.

The way he moved was like an invitation to pure pleasure. That tight ass begged to be kneaded, caressed and subjected to all sorts of other sinful delights. She took the opportunity to ogle the lush vision before her freely. She had known he was gorgeous the night before, though with the dark lighting and the alcohol affecting her senses, she hadn't truly appreciated him to his full yummy extent.

The afternoon sun highlighted his blond hair, showing off the varying shades from a wheat color to darker red-tinted strands. His skin, tanned a light golden hue, seemed to absorb the sun rather than reflect it. He was large with thick, bulging muscles, but not exaggeratedly so. He was the perfect size to wrap around both her and Zander.

The image of the three of them entangled in a mass of naked arms and legs flashed briefly in her mind, the impact powerful enough that she couldn't stop the moan that was pulled from deep inside her. The walls of her sex clenched in a tantalizing rhythm that matched her increased pulse. Marco turned and replaced his cell in the clip on his hip. She felt each step he took closer to her as a deep, penetrating throb within her core.

Returning to the table, he extended a hand to her. "Ready?"

Oh hell yes, she was ready. She was more than ready to lick every inch of that sun-kissed skin, and beyond ready to have every ounce of his power above her, inside her and devouring her. She swallowed hard, licking at her dry lips. She was so fucking ready she yearned for it in every cell of her body.

"Where are we going?" she asked curiously as she took his hand without hesitation and allowed him to pull her to her feet.

Marco chuckled, threw some bills on the table to cover his wine and started leading her out of Posey's. "Somewhere I can impress you, of course."

What she really wanted to know were answers to the important questions like, were clothes required and would she be too exhausted to work tomorrow? If the answers were no, she could suggest some alterations to his plans that would have them both unfit to rise from bed for days. She didn't ask the question out loud, just not brave enough yet. She was feeling bolder the more time she spent with them, but it was still too new. She had some serious doubts in her ability to ask for what she wanted without dying of embarrassment, but, damn it, she was going to give it her all, very soon.

Her earlier fantasies of dark hair and a lean body doing skillfully naughty things to her body were burned into Symone's head. Hell, she could still taste Zander on her lips. That was the funny thing about fantasy — it could change in the blink of an eye.

As she strolled down Main Street, her hand in Marco's, those fantasies grew and expanded into some amazingly wicked places. Marco was gorgeous enough to make some very happy fantasies all on his own. He was pure male heat and strength.

The air around him sparked with confidence but he wasn't cocky in the least. The way her body quivered inside, it obviously remembered just how that body moved against hers. It wanted more. Instead of replacing the seared images of Zander in her mind, Marco was right in the thick of those naughty dreams along with her and Zander. It was warm out, yet the heat inside Symone was an inferno. Good God, what would it be like to be the sole focus of both of them? At the same time no less. The jolt of lust that rocketed through her was so powerful, her steps faltered.

Marco pulled her to him before she could face plant on the sidewalk. "Whoa there, sweets. You okay?" He held her until she was no longer in danger of falling and wrapped an arm around her waist.

Being closer to his body and feeling his strong arms around her was so not helping. That jolt decided to head straight to her center.

Control. You're the seductress. He is our prey.

Easy for that annoying little voice to say, it didn't have to deal with the physical aspects. The stupid bitch just shut down when things got to intense.

It's been six months. Give me a bit of a break here. I'm beyond horny, okay?

Great! Now she was arguing with herself. If she didn't find some kind of outlet for the pent-up sexual frustration she would go mad.

"I'm fine, just wasn't paying attention to where I was walking. You gonna tell me where we're headed?" She tried to focus on something other than her rising libido.

"Curious little thing, aren't you?" Marco chuckled as he urged her to continue down the sidewalk.

"Yeah, well, I'm not a cat so no danger there. I am going to an unknown place, with someone I barely know. You can see why I may be a little questioning."

"You're in the great big county of Wakulla and you're in public, so hush and let me impress you." He glanced over at her and arched an eyebrow. "You're not one of those who hates surprises, are you?"

"Oh, I love surprises," she said honestly. "Not the kind that finds me face down in the gutter and a date with a stainless steel slab, though."

Marco tilted his head back and laughed. "You watch too much TV, Symone. Either that or you need to cut back on the mystery books you're reading. First of all there are no alleys in Wakulla, and secondly"—he moved in to whisper in her ear—"your body is to be worshiped and pleasured, not abused."

The tingling sensation along her spine increased with Marco's warm breath and innuendos.

You are so not helping me get these fantasies under control. She groaned silently.

After walking another block, Marco stopped outside Creative Creations. "Here we are. See, no alleys." He opened the door and ushered her inside.

Creative Creations was an eclectic mix of art from local artists. The walls were covered in amazing works that would rival any New York exhibition. The shop had everything from abstract art to fantasy, landscape, modern and fine nude art right down to a display of local elementary students' work. It was one of her favorite places. Every time she visited, there was something new to explore and enjoy.

"Hey, Maggie," Marco greeted the shop's owner as he stepped up to the counter. "Is my room set up?"

"Oh my God, you're right, she is stunning." Maggie pushed past Marco and practically bounced toward Symone with her hand outstretched. "You must be Symone. I'm Maggie. I can't wait to display your painting."

Symone took the offered hand and shook it, a little dazed by Maggie's enthusiasm. She was a tiny little thing, probably in her mid-fifties to early sixties given the amount of laugh lines around her twinkling eyes, yet she sure didn't dress the part. Maggie looked as if she'd just stepped out of a picture from Woodstock. Her long salt-and-pepper hair was parted in the middle and tied back with a simple band, and small white flowers had been placed randomly around the crown of her head. A tie-dyed T-shirt, long flowing gauze skirt and sandals completed her look.

"My painting?" Symone asked, turning to look at Marco.

Marco stepped up laughing and put an arm around Maggie. "It was kind of a surprise, Mags."

Maggie released Symone's hand and playfully swatted at Marco. "Oops. Surprise," she said as she ducked under his arm and returned to the counter.

"You paint?" Symone asked Marco, intrigued. With his build, she would have guessed his hobbies would have been more sports related. His large hands seemed built for power, not delicate strokes of a brush.

Marco shrugged, looking embarrassed. "Yeah, a little."

Maggie returned and handed Marco a large leather portfolio and a small box of pencils. "He's too modest. He's an amazing artist." She grabbed Symone's hand and pulled her to a wall. "See for yourself."

The nudes on display were stunning. They were depictions of women and men in various poses. He'd discreetly covered the model's more private areas by either positioning them just right or using articles of discarded clothing or fabrics. They were erotic and yet left just enough to the imagination. "These are amazing," Symone said in awe.

"Thanks," he replied, sounding almost shy.

She got a glimpse at a completely different side of him in just that one spoken word. The man was gorgeous, powerful in build, and while she knew he wasn't cocky, it was the shyness that was unexpected. This side of Marco made her chest feel a little tight and she forced herself to push it away.

Looking over her shoulder at him and noticing his cheeks were a little pink from her compliment, she asked, "You're going to paint me?" She suddenly felt a little self-conscious. As magnificent as the paintings were, she wasn't so sure she wanted to be displayed in all her naked glory.

"C'mon," he said as he headed down the hall toward the back of the shop "I'm not going to ask you to take your clothes off."

Relief surged through her as she followed him down the hall, then she shuddered when he added, "This time."

Symone was laid out on the chaise longue, her stomach knotted and her heart racing along at a snappy beat. The soft brush of Marco's fingers against her skin as he arranged her dress to his liking was sending her libido past rising and straight into the sphere of boiling. The hungry look in his eyes as he appraised her proved she wasn't the only one feeling the heat between them.

"Perfect," he murmured in a husky voice. He picked up a sketchpad and pencil and took a seat across from her.

He'd positioned her with both hands above her head. One foot on the floor, the other leg stretched out the length of the lounge. Her dress was pushed up to expose her thighs and the bodice pulled down and barely covered her swollen nipples. Symone licked her lips and tried her damnedest not to squirm. As his eyes continued to take in every inch of her, every look was like a kiss to her skin, a soft, delicate caress of heat that made it increasingly more difficult to hold still.

"Are you a full-time artist?" She needed to shift his intense focus away from her.

"Nah, I just do it for fun and fear of Mag's whip." He didn't look up from his sketch.

"Not into the kinky scene, huh?" she teased.

He immediately looked up at her with heavy-lidded eyes. "Oh, I love kinky." His voice was husky, emphasizing his statement, and she felt the rumbling sound deep inside her. He returned his attention back to his work. "Maggie and a whip are not my idea of kinky," he chuckled.

I so want to know your kinks. Any chance they include you, me and Zander?

She couldn't ask that, but damn she wanted to know. "What do you do for a living then?"

"My dad owns a construction company. I've pretty much worked for him my whole life. Hell, I can't remember a time when I wasn't either building shit or tearing it down. I think I came out of the womb with a hammer in my hand. He wants more time to travel, so I've been taking over the management side of it lately. I'm not real fond of it. I'd much rather be out with the guys using my hands, but I'm an only child and he doesn't trust anyone but family to run it." He shrugged without looking up.

"The fantasy was starting to build of you in tight jeans and denim shirt. Hot and sweaty, covered in sawdust, and you ruined it with the pencil-pusher image," she teased lightly.

"I still get hot and sweaty." He looked up at her, his eyes heated. "Maybe we can come up with something other than sawdust to cover me in."

Symone's heart pounded and her mouth went dry with anticipation of seeing this gorgeous man hot and sweaty and…

Easy, girl, breathe. She took a deep breath and ripped her gaze away from his. She focused on the sketchpad and took a couple more inhales. "Where did you learn to paint?"

Marco chuckled and returned his eyes back to the sketch. "My mom was a painter. She created the most beautiful landscapes. From as early as I can remember, we always had our easels side by side, putting on art shows for my dad." His voice took on a melancholy tone. "She died when I was sixteen."

"I'm so sorry. She was obviously a wonderful teacher."

"Thanks. I like to think so."

They fell into a comfortable silence while Marco continued to sketch. The serious conversation banked some of her lust for the moment. As the minutes ticked by, Marco seemed to go into a trance. He nibbled at his bottom lip and his brows furrowed in concentration as he drew. Watching him bite at that bottom lip, she wanted nothing more than to lick and soothe the abused flesh. Kiss away the deep lines between his brows.

The sedate feeling from their conversation didn't last long as she continued to watch him work. Soon her thoughts turned to kissing her way down that handsome face, inhaling his fresh woodsy scent as she licked and kissed a trail down his throat to that hard, muscular chest. Pluck and nip at his nipples until they were as tight and erect as hers were becoming.

"What are you thinking about?" Marco asked, his tone knowing.

Symone snapped her gaze back up to his face and met his mischievous hazel eyes. "Uh… Well… I was just wondering how your sketch was coming along." She tried to hide her embarrassment at being caught losing herself in the thought of him.

"Mmmhmm. You must be really excited to see it," he pointed out with a quiet laugh. "You're breathing fast, and I take it the flushed skin and slight trembling is from anticipation and excitement to see my sketch?"

Busted. Damn, what did he expect? The man was gorgeous. With little else to do but lay back and admire him, how could she help it? "Are you going to let me see what's got you biting on your lip?"

Marco stood and approached the couch. "I'd rather show you." He leaned down and placed a soft kiss on the exposed skin just above her right breast.

Symone slid her fingers through his soft blond locks, as a moan rose from deep inside her at the brush of his lips against her chest. The contact set in motion a domino effect in her nerve endings and raced along each one until converging between her thighs. She gasped at the powerful sensation as he looked up and met her eyes from beneath thick lashes. "Oh God," she moaned.

"Are you sure it's *just* the drawing you're excited about?" he asked as he moved up until his lips met hers.

Symone licked at that abused lower lip, provoking a small groan from Marco, then reluctantly released him. She knew if she let the kiss go any further, she wouldn't be able to hold back until she devoured him. The last thing she needed was Maggie to come to check Marco's progress and find her attacking the man. But, Christ, how she wanted to. It took every ounce of willpower she could muster to place her hands against his chest and push instead of pull him until she felt his full weight against her. "Impress me," she whispered.

Marco sat next to her and gave her a pouty look. "I was trying to but you pushed me away." He handed her the sketchpad.

She was going to come back with some snappy reply but the words died as she took in Marco's sketch. It was breathtaking. He had created such a realistic depiction of her. It looked as if the image of her could stand up and step off the page. "Wow! This is stunning."

"I had a great model," he replied nonchalantly.

She sat up and clutched the drawing. She couldn't take her eyes from it. "No really, Marco, this is absolutely astounding. You're very talented."

He leaned in closer and whispered, "Are you impressed?"

Was he kidding? The man was not only gorgeous and sweet but he was talented as hell. She looked up into those stunning hazel eyes and nodded. "I'm more than impressed."

"Good. I want to do more than impress you." Just as he leaned closer, Maggie chose that moment to walk in.

"How's it going? I gotta close up and get home... Oops, sorry to interrupt."

Marco winked at Symone and stood up. "It's okay, Maggie, we were just finishing up."

"Oh, let me see." Maggie squealed when Symone handed her the sketch. "Your best work yet. I know you're going to let me display this one, aren't you?"

Marco went to the small sink, washed his hands as he laughed. "You say that every time."

"That's because it's true. You just keep getting better and better."

Marco seemed to puff up at Maggie's praise. He shook his head, then dried his hands and began gathering up his supplies. "You'll have to ask Symone. It belongs to her."

"You're giving it to me?" Symone gasped.

Marco met her gaze. "Of course. I still have to paint it but it's yours when I'm done."

Symone jumped up and practically threw herself at Marco. His big arms wrapped around her instantly, lifted her off her feet. He held her tight against him, and she kissed him soundly.

"Thank you!" She was breathless as her excitement from not only the gift, but from how his body felt against hers, surged through her.

"Damn. If that's the kind of reaction I can expect I'll be sure to draw you one every day."

Maggie slapped Marco on the back. "Don't even think about it, young man," she chastised. "Find another way to get that reaction. Unless you plan to find time for me in that busy schedule. I need new prints for my shop."

"Yes, Madam Whip-wielder," Marco snorted.

Maggie headed to the door, sketch in hand. "I'll put this up with the other ones you need to paint," she said as she stepped out of the room.

Marco let Symone down slowly. The full length of his body slid against hers until he set her on her feet. Lust swept through her as his hard bulge pressed against her stomach. They stared at each other. Both breathed harder as the bands of arousal chained them together.

"Very impressed," she moaned as her body involuntarily pushed further against that hard shaft.

Marco responded by tightening his grip on her and rolling his hips. "You haven't seen anything yet," he growled. The barely controlled sound increased the eroticism his body was creating as it moved against hers. "But you will."

"Are you two coming?" Maggie called out from the front of the shop, breaking the carnal spell they had fallen under.

The first response that popped into her head at Maggie's question had some of the tension leaving her body, causing her to giggle. Had Maggie given them just a couple of more minutes she might have been able to answer with a little more enthusiasm — with a *Yes, oh God yes, I'm coming*.

Groaning in obvious frustration, Marco released her and ran his fingers through his hair, mussing it. He really was quite adorable with his mouth drawn into a pout and his hair disheveled. Her smile turned to a wince for Marco's obvious discomfort as he adjusted the front of his pants with a pained look on his face.

Then again, it couldn't be any more painful than her sorely denied body. Stupid self-imposed chastity.

Hopefully, she wouldn't have to wait to find out what Marco meant by his declaration of *'But you will'*.

She'd explode if she had to wait too long.

Chapter Five

Not one sale in over three weeks, now everyone in the flippin' country wanted to look at a house in Tallahassee.

Symone knew she shouldn't complain. If the deals went through on the four homes she had purchase agreements on, she was going to have one hell of a sweet commission check. Problem was, her body didn't give a rat's ass about commissions, home inspections or anything else having to do with business. It wanted out of its celibate hell.

After dropping her keys on the coffee table, she made her way to the kitchen, grabbed a soda out of the fridge and flung herself on the couch. The long hours she was putting in at work weren't the only thing causing her exhaustion.

The damn sexy men and their late night calls added to it. Marco and Zander were now going for the record of who could send her to the loony bin the quickest. Their damn suggestive banter and sexy voices every night before bed had led to some hot as hell dreams, both of them playing a starring role. She snickered as she sipped her soda.

Wouldn't they be a little taken aback to know what they were doing in her naughty night-time shows? Here they were trying to see who could win her over, outdo the other and all she could think about was having them both at the same time. There was no way in hell she could choose between them.

At this point in her life, she didn't want to choose one or the other. It was easier to see them as objects of pleasure to indulge in when she thought of them together, rather than individuals. Each of them sparked something in her.

Zander with his exotic good looks and wonderful intellect not only stimulated her body but her mind as well. On the other hand, Marco was sweet, almost shy sometimes. He had the body and look of a linebacker, yet he was soft and tender, funny, not to mention one hell of a talented artist. Therein lay one of her biggest problems. Well, second biggest problem if she included physical ones.

With her history of always giving her heart to the wrong man, she just didn't trust herself. She had no clue how men and some women were able to view sex as purely an unemotional, meaningless, physical urge that needed to be filled, but, damn it, she was going to do her best to find out.

The feeling that she had done something wrong to deserve such poor treatment or was lacking in some way was something she didn't want to deal with anymore. Never again would she let someone take her for granted, cheat on her and make her think it was her fault. Oh hell no! She was young, independent, open-minded, and fuck anyone who thought otherwise.

This was her time to shine. To take what she wanted, when she wanted and consequences be damned. "The new and improved Symone Adams is loud, proud and on the prowl. Ladies, lock up your husbands, your boyfriends, your..."

Laughter overtook her and due to the very real risk of having her soda snort out of her nose, she forced her thoughts away from such silliness. Though she could easily admit that being silly combined with the physical needs of her body made holding back her emotions a little easier to bear.

As much as one part of her wanted more than anything to let the shield around her heart slip, she just couldn't. She was scared shitless to think about how much she liked both of them as real people. Fear of heartache helped with her new resolve and today was going to be a test of just how well she held up and stayed true to her new attitude. Today she would be getting up close and personal with the two men that she tried desperately to keep at arm's length emotionally, while hoping to indulge in them physically.

She should blame them for the predicament she was in and the early test. When Sedesa had invited her to her backyard barbeque and pool party, then told her to bring a date, she hadn't planned on inviting either one.

Somehow while her defenses were down, again their fault, she might have mentioned something about the party to each of them. How could she be blamed that she had somehow ended up with two dates for the same party?

"Ha! That's all there is to it. It's their fault," she declared with conviction.

That's my story and I'm sticking to it. She set her soda down and headed to the bedroom to change.

They'd basically invited themselves to the party. It couldn't be her fault if they didn't like who was in attendance. They should have asked who was on the guest list before committing to it, right? Yet, as she pulled out her bathing suit and shorts, she just didn't think such an argument was going to fly with those two. Then again, she knew how competitive they were. They were probably in cahoots together.

God, I hope so.

She slipped on the string bikini and studied the shorts she had chosen before throwing them back on the bed. They were cute but she wasn't going for that today. Maybe if she kept them off balance with her attire they wouldn't have time to notice the other one was there.

Yeah right. It was hard not to notice either one of them.

She grabbed a sheer cover-up and slipped it on over her suit. She wasn't really sure why it was called a cover-up, it certainly didn't cover up much of anything at all.

Perfect.

She piled her hair up in a twist, refreshed her waterproof makeup and grabbed her beach bag and keys. Before heading out, she grabbed the bottle of Captain Morgan's coconut rum off the counter. If things went badly with Marco and Zander she could still enjoy a few Pissing Parrots. A couple of those and she wouldn't care who was at the party. She'd be too drunk to care.

As she pulled up in front of Sedesa's place, her heart went into rapid beating mode and her palms started to sweat. Symone cut the engine and took a few deep breaths while she tried to muster up the nerve she'd need to set her new resolution into motion.

This is what you wanted.

Get them together, to seduce and have her wicked way with them. Make some of her private desires come to life.

I can do this.

Hell, she wanted to do this. She took one more deep breath then grabbed the rum and stepped out of the car. She relaxed a little when she didn't notice either Marco's or Zander's cars. If she hurried, maybe she could get down one of those Pissing Pirates before they showed up. There was a lot to be said for liquid courage at times like this.

"Hey, Sedesa," she called out as she stepped through the front door.

"In the kitchen. Hurry!" came her muffled reply.

Symone darted into the kitchen, uncertain about what she was getting into. But the distress in Sedesa's tone had her on high alert. She scanned the area, frantically searching for her best friend. When she found her, she burst out laughing.

Sedesa's head was deep inside one of the bottom cupboards, her hands pressed against the opening as she struggled to pull herself free.

"What the hell are you doing?"

"Stop laughing and get me out of here," Sedesa complained as she continued to struggle. "My hair is stuck."

"This is a very interesting situation we have here," she teased. "I can't wait to see this video on YouTube."

"You wouldn't dare!" Sedesa screeched. "Get me out of here. I swear if you take one fucking picture I'll plaster your college graduation pictures all over Facebook. Damn it, Symone, get me out of here."

That got her moving. She knew Sedesa was not talking about the cap and gown pictures but the ones from the party afterward. It had been bad enough that she couldn't remember a single thing from that night once the party had moved to the bar. When forced to look at the pictures the next day, they were…

Well, needless to say, they were not for those with any preconceived notions of how a *lady* was supposed to behave. It had been more like good girls gone wild. At least she hadn't flashed her tits or removed any of her clothing, so she'd been told, and so far there hadn't been any photographic or video image to prove otherwise. The memory of her dancing on the bar, though, flashed in her head, and to this day was still at the top of her most embarrassing moments ever. Shaking her head, she helped free Sedesa.

It took screaming and threats of permanent bodily injury but Symone finally got her hair free from the tracks of the drawer without having to resort to cutting her hair. "What the hell were you doing in there anyway?"

Sedesa sat on the floor, trying to put her disheveled hair back up in its clip. "I was looking for a platter."

"And you had to crawl inside…"

"Shut up and help me up," Sedesa interrupted with a pout. "The kitchen is not my friend. You know that."

Symone pulled her to her feet. As soon as their eyes met, they both cracked up laughing. The kitchen, laundry room and cleaning supplies were never Sedesa's friends. Just the thought sent Symone into further laughter, uncontrolled snorts and hiccups.

It had also given her something other than her tightly wound nerves to concentrate on. That was until the thought caught her attention again, sending her mood right back to somber. She knew exactly how to rectify that.

She wiped the tears from her eyes and headed for the cupboard for a glass. She took out two tall ones, and set them on the counter and looked at Sedesa expectantly. "Please tell me you have 7-Up and cranberry schnapps or I'm turning my ass right around and heading home."

"I take it you didn't choose?" She pointed toward the small door. "7-Up is in the pantry." Sedesa snorted as she set a bottle of schnapps on the counter next to her.

Symone grabbed the soda from the pantry and brought it back. "You tell me how the hell I'm supposed to choose? Besides," she continued as she mixed two drinks. "I've decided that this is their fault entirely. They caught me at a weak moment and coaxed me into an invite. Hell, I didn't even invite them. I only mentioned where I would be. Might have given them an address." She looked at the disbelieving look on Sedesa's face. "Oh, shut up, it's their fault."

"Uh-huh," Sedesa giggled as she accepted the drink. "I can imagine that one of them would be enough to make me go weak. The two of them together"—she raised her glass and clicked it against Symone's—"would knock me on my ass. And I do mean that in the best possible way. Cheers."

Her good mood returned as they enjoyed their drinks. Just being around Sedesa eased her panic. Friends since they'd been fourteen, they always knew what the other was feeling and what they needed. They had graduated high school and college together. When Symone had informed Sedesa she was moving to Florida, the only thing she had asked was when were *they* were leaving. It had been as easy as that, both of them loading all their meager belongings into a rented U-Haul and never looking back.

She helped Sedesa get the rest of the snacks out and ice down the sodas and beer while she fought a precarious battle with her nerves. Finally, they were under control for the moment.

A couple of Sedesa's co-workers, Carol and Leah, Sedesa's current man, Ian, and Todd from next door had shown up just as they'd finished setting up for the party. She chatted with Carol about this and that, but she really wasn't paying attention. She was too busy watching for new arrivals.

She had just downed the last of her liquid courage at the same instance a deep baritone voice behind her had her nearly choking on her drink. *Ah hell, here we go.* Symone forced a casual smile on her face, which took an even greater effort to maintain when she turned around. *Shit.* Obviously, Marco and Zander's clocks were set to the same time, down to the minute.

Symone groaned silently as she walked over to greet them. The jangle of nerves caused her step to be a little shaky but she trudged on with her big fake smile. Marco's annoyed exhalation as Zander muttered something she couldn't make out greeted her.

From the harsh scowl on Zander's face, she knew he wasn't telling him he was happy to see him again. Both looked tense and she swore she could hear Marco's teeth grind as he fought to hold back his response as she stepped up beside them.

"Hi, guys. Glad you could make it." She bit her lip as both men's gaze dropped from her face and down her body. The comical response of their eyes going wide and a huff of breath escaping their parted lips would have been hilarious under normal circumstances. No, come to think of it, it was hilarious and she couldn't hold back the laugh that burst out.

Marco's eyes narrowed as he glanced quickly at Zander then back at her. "I didn't realize you'd invited him." He jerked a thumb at him as if she would need clarification as to whom he meant.

"Well, actually…"

"What's the matter, Polo? Not happy to see me?" Zander asked without taking his eyes from her, and she was sure Marco hadn't missed the sarcastic tone.

"Oh, I'm happy to see someone all right." Marco stepped up close, and leaned in to place a kiss on Symone's lips. "Christ, you look amazing." He put an arm around her waist and looked back at Zander over his shoulder. "I'll be ecstatic when I see you leave."

She hugged Marco back and returned the kiss. "Be nice," she whispered against his lips then pulled away.

"Yeah, you just want to stare at my ass." Zander shot back as he pushed past Marco and hugged Symone. "He's right about one thing, though. You do look amazing. Thanks for inviting me."

The press of his lips against hers was sweet but the proprietary hand against her back made it clear he had no intention to step aside for Marco. She returned the hug briefly and once again stepped back.

She shot a look at Marco and interrupted him before he could respond to Zander's taunt. "Thanks, but as I was saying…" She met each of their gazes before continuing, "I didn't actually invite either one of you." She chuckled at the agitated look they gave one another. "But I'm glad you're both here. C'mon, I'll introduce you two to everyone and find you something to drink. I hope you're hungry."

Later, after introductions had been made and they'd all enjoyed an amazing barbeque, Symone found herself lounging next to the pool with Zander on one side of her and Marco on the other.

Sedesa had instantly lost herself in Ian and they were currently playing kissy face on the other side of the pool. She really didn't have anything in common or know Sedesa's co-workers that well and it hadn't taken long for everyone to split into their own little groups. Obviously, her *little* group was the sexy men flanking her. The boys had teased back and forth good-heartedly but she knew underneath that many of the taunts were not jokes. They seemed to relax a bit with each other, at least the looks that could kill had stopped and they'd both seemed a little less tense. For the moment, she wasn't in any imminent danger of being in the middle of testosterone gone wild but she wasn't holding out hope that it would last.

As she basked in the afternoon sun, she contemplated her current situation. All she had wanted to do was go out, find some new hot stud to help end her long drought and maybe have a few laughs. She wasn't looking for anything serious and still wasn't, but for fuck's sake, how was she going to bring her celibacy to an end when she couldn't choose between them?

The better question was how to get them to stop jockeying for top position and accept a compromise? With the hellish week she'd had at work there hadn't been any opportunities with either one of them except chats on the phone. Oh, and what those calls had inspired. The image of both of them wrapped around her filled her thoughts. Their gorgeous bodies slick with sweat as they worked in perfect unison to bring her pleasure. Their hands, lips and tongues explored every inch of her body. A convolution of desire wove its way along her skin to pool low in her belly as the image became more vivid. A deep ache caused her to flush.

"You're starting to get a little pink," Zander muttered. "Better let me put some sunblock on you."

Symone's eyes snapped open and she turned to look at Zander rising from his lounge chair. She couldn't see his eyes, since they were hidden behind his dark shades, but the grin on his face told her he'd been watching her and knew the flush on her skin had little to do with the sun. He picked up the sunscreen and put a large dollop in his palms. Symone was riveted to those strong hands rubbing together. Her body began to tingle in anticipation of feeling them caress her skin. The instant he touched her shoulder, she jerked at the jolt of arousal that raced through her.

"It's not cold, is it?" Zander asked, knowing that it was, as he began to massage the lotion down her arm.

Symone shook her head in response.

"Let me give you a hand," Marco offered as he grabbed the lotion and poured a small line down her shin.

Zander watched, enthralled as goosebumps erupted across Symone's skin when the cold liquid touched her heated flesh. The moan that passed her lips as they worked lotion into her skin was music to his ears.

As he slid his hands toward her chest and Marco moved his up her thighs, Symone shifted, pushing up against their caresses.

Fuck, she's gorgeous.

Zander longed to follow the same path as his hands were taking with his tongue. His mouth watered as he imagined licking every inch of perfection in front of him. Even the sight of Marco's hands on her heightened his desire, and he was shocked the stirring of jealousy that he usually felt toward Marco was absent. He wasn't sure what that meant and refused to think about it too deeply. He would simply follow his instincts.

Since the day they'd walked the beach, he'd been itching to get his hands on Symone, so he ignored any concerns he might have and concentrated on the silky smoothness of her skin. Only the knowledge that there were others present kept him in check. The small whimpers and soft moans coming from Symone were making that task increasingly difficult, though.

As his fingers brushed across the swells of her breasts, he was almost convinced that the other guests were insignificant. Hard nipples pressing against the top of her suit were shredding his hard-fought restraint. When he couldn't stand it another second, he growled. "Roll over." *Damn! A man can only handle so much temptation.*

"Got to make sure we don't miss any spots," Marco said, his tone husky as he pressed against her legs, encouraging her to roll. Zander was certain Marco's mind had been wandering down the same path.

"This isn't necessary, guys. I never burn." But she didn't hesitate to comply.

"There's always a first time. I wouldn't be able to forgive myself if I let this delicate skin burn."

Zander bristled at Marco's bullshit declaration. "I'm sure that's the only thing going through that thick skull of yours, Polo."

"Since you can read my mind then I won't even have to say fuck off out loud, will I?"

"Nope, got that too," Zander chuckled.

Symone jerked again as they poured cold lotion onto her thighs and back. She moved away from the sensation and seconds later pushed back against their hands when they began to rub in the cream. He could feel her body tremble with the effort. He stilled his hands as he raked his eyes up and down her body, mesmerized by the sight of the round globes of her tight bottom and the sounds escaping her.

It took a great deal of concentration for him to focus on applying the sunblock. He moved his hands gently across the heated skin of her back, the muscles moving and shifting under his touch, drawing him in. His hard shaft throbbed painfully in the confines of his shorts. He discreetly stole a glance at Marco and instantly realized the man was fighting the same battle, if the tent of his shorts was any indication.

To Zander's horror, his body responded to the sight before him. A wave of lust rocked through him and left him dizzy.

What the fuck?

No way. He couldn't be turned on by…a man. He shifted his eyes away and promptly blanked his alarm. He convinced himself it was a combination of a lack of bed partner lately, the feel and sounds of Symone, and that the heat of the afternoon that was affecting him. He focused his attention back on the luscious creature sprawled out on the lounger but it did little to stem the flow of arousal that was surging through him.

Marco's hands slid up Symone's thigh. The movement of her hips increased as she lost herself to the attention they showered her with. He gave in to the urge to taste her. He leaned down and pressed his lips against the nape of her neck and brushed his hands along her back, down to her sweet ass. Every screaming nerve felt the effects of her flavor on his lips, and he groaned at the intensity of it. He snaked his tongue out, trying to capture more of her essence. He slid his fingertips beneath her bikini bottom and he massaged the mounds of her ass. Symone bucked her hips as she moaned in bliss.

Zander looked up and met Marco's hungry gaze and a jolt shot straight through his dick, settling in his balls. *No! No fucking way am I coming in my goddamn shorts.*

Marco's gaze flicked toward the pool and in an unspoken agreement, they moved. He couldn't say who hit the water first, didn't really care. All he cared about was that as he dove into the cool water it had the desired effect. The danger of shooting in his trunks like a teenage boy was no longer at critical mass.

The sudden loss of contact, the loud splash and droplets of cold water on her back had Symone jumping up and yelping. "Jesus Christ!"

She turned just as both Marco and Zander bobbed up out of the water. "What the hell was that all about?" she asked, frustrated. Wincing, she grabbed a towel and started drying off her overly sensitive body.

Marco made his way to the edge of the pool, folded his arms on the rim and rested his chin on his forearms. "It was getting a little warm." He winked. "I was beginning to worry about heat stroke."

She glared at Zander as he moved up next to Marco. "You too?"

Heat stroke? Really? Try spontaneous human combustion, buddy!

He shook his head, water droplets spraying Marco. "Nah, thought Polo here had lost his mind. Just making sure his lard ass didn't sink to the bottom."

Marco arched an eyebrow at him. "Lard ass?" he asked incredulously. "I'll show you lard ass." Marco dove on top of Zander and a new battle was on.

Even with the painful ache still gripping her body she couldn't help but laugh as they tried to outdo the other. They wrestled, laughing and taunting one another as they tried to force the other under the water. She was relieved they seemed to be getting along but her body was still a little pissed that they were showing each other attention instead of her. She shook her head at their antics and went in search of another Pissing Parrot.

Chapter Six

The sun was just beginning to set and although the heat of the day was beginning to wane the air was still thick with humidity and registering in the mid-eighties.

Symone eyed the pool. It looked refreshing. Her skin felt tight from the hours in the sun. She eyed it again and shook her head. It might be calling to her but after the second Pissing Parrot and a shot of Hot Damn!, she seriously doubted if she'd be able to make her arms and legs work well enough to keep her afloat. Maybe a better idea would be to head home and settle for a cool shower. Lord knew she needed it. The Florida sun wasn't the only thing that had been heating her up today.

Once Marco and Zander had finished their game of chicken in the pool, they actually seemed to get along. That's not to say they still weren't in heavy competition with the other but the tone of it had become more playful than serious. Their current endeavor was to see who could eat the last of the snacks and the remaining barbeque.

Damn those boys could eat. At least Sedesa wouldn't have to worry about what to do with leftovers. Her stomach rolled, feeling a little nauseated at the thought of food, a clear sign that she'd had enough to drink and should really think seriously about that cool shower.

"Hey, Symone. Great party, huh?"

Symone looked up to see Sedesa's neighbor, Todd, standing over her. "Yeah, Sedesa always knows how to throw a good one. How've you been?"

Todd was a thirty-something accountant. Hell of a nice guy but he was the stereotypical finance geek. He was an inch shorter than Symone and probably about the same weight. He wore his hair short, parted on the side. Wire-rimmed glasses sat on his button nose. He was cute in that nerdy kind of way, always dressed in starched white button-up shirts and either dress slacks or dress shorts. Whenever she was around him, she had to fight the urge to unbutton his top button and ruffle his hair. She never gave in to the urge since she knew Todd had a crush on her and did not want to encourage him. It was tempting, though. He was absolutely adorable when he blushed. She pulled her feet up under her and motioned to the foot of her lounge. "Have a seat."

There was that adorable blush.

"Thanks." He sat where she had indicated but didn't meet her gaze. "So um... Well, I was wondering..." He fumbled over his words as he glanced over to where Marco and Zander were still waging war on the snack table.

"You want to know which one is my date?" she asked.

Todd peeked up at her and his face went a deeper shade of red before he nodded.

"Actually, neither of them. They both kind of wormed their way into an invite." She lowered her voice to a loud whisper. "Which one do you think I should choose?"

Todd glanced once again at the guys then met her gaze. His ears went bright red. "Both are hot, I'll take whichever one you don't."

Well, I'll be damned. Here she'd thought his shyness and stuttering was because he was crushing on her. She couldn't help herself and started to laugh. "Okay, though I may just keep them both."

Todd's laughter joined hers and he seemed to relax some. "Greedy much?"

Her eyes landed on Marco, taking in his large, masculine frame, then at Zander, the exotic stallion. Greedy wasn't the half of it. "Wouldn't you be?" she asked conspiratorially.

"Oh yeah," Todd replied dreamily as he followed her gaze. "I'm a numbers kind of guy and those two multiplied by me—oh, my frickin' God."

Symone snapped her head back toward Todd. The look on his face was pure hunger and lust. "Why, you naughty boy, who would have guessed under that geek façade was a little tiger." She snorted.

He shrugged, his lips twitching in an effort to keep a straight face. "Don't let the outward appearances fool you. Underneath I have a very large...*portfolio.*"

Symone cracked up, and Todd joined in.

She was still laughing and had to wipe the tears from her eyes when Marco and Zander made their way closer. Both she and Todd met each other's eyes. The laughter intensified until they were both holding on to their stomachs and fighting to breathe.

"Okay I'm thinking that it's time for Miss Giggles here to call it a night. What do you think, Polo?" Zander asked.

"I'd say so," Marco replied without even commenting on the teasing nickname. He had to be getting used to it or at least chose to ignore it. "You ready, Symone?"

She gave them each a bleary look as the laughter faded to soft giggles. "Depends what you're offering."

Todd nudged her with his elbow. "Okay, time for me to head home. Alone," he said with a mock pout as he stood.

That was all it took, and Symone started laughing again.

"Upsie daisy," Marco muttered as he took her arm and helped her to her feet. She was a little unsteady — a combination of the alcohol and the amusement that still had hold of her.

Symone hugged Todd and wished him a good night before turning to the guys. "Okay, which one of you is going to drive me home?"

"I am," their confident replies came at the same time.

"Oh, hell no you're not, Zoo-man, you had three beers, and no way are you getting behind the wheel with this prize." Marco moved up and put an arm around Symone's shoulders.

Zander pushed off Marco's arm and replaced it with his. "I had two beers over the last six hours and tons of food. I doubt I'd even register on a blow."

Marco shoved at Zander's arm but he held on. Marco glared at Zander for a moment then placed his arm around her waist. "I had one so I'll drive her car and you can follow us."

"Guys, guys, I'm standing right here. I'm an adult for God's sake and I can take myself home." Actually, she was a little too tipsy to be driving but she could always crawl into one of Sedesa's spare rooms and sleep it off. She didn't suggest it, though, as they ignored her statement and began leading her toward the front yard. She was rather comfortable right where she was. Their arms wrapped around her felt like the most natural thing in the world. It felt right. It was also setting her nerve endings alight with desire. Sandwiched between them, knowing they were taking her home...

What the hell do I have to fight against or complain about? Oh yes, boys, take me home.

She started to giggle again. "Bye, Sedesa," she yelled over her shoulder.

"Where are your keys?" Marco inquired as they stepped up to her car.

"Oh those." She had to stop and think about it for a minute. She knew she had keys somewhere. After all, she'd driven here. She started to giggle again. "Keys?"

"Yes, Symone, keys. You know the little metal things you use to turn on your car?" Zander teased.

"Umm... Oh yeah, those. They're on the kitchen counter."

"I'll grab them," Zander offered and headed back into the house.

"You sure you're okay?" Marco pulled her into an embrace.

She snuggled in, loving the feel of him against her. His scent surrounded her. "I am now."

Marco tilted her head back with the tip of one finger. "I like that," he murmured then kissed her softly.

It may have been tender and gentle but it curled her toes. The press of his mouth was an invitation, one she greedily accepted. She licked at his lips, encouraging him to open. Marco accepted the offer and devoured her mouth. He kneaded her ass and pulled her closer.

A thrill ran down her spine as the hard bulge of his shaft pressed against her stomach. He explored her mouth just as thoroughly as his hands explored her flesh. Each pass of his hands caused her hips to rock, creating a delicious friction. She wanted to crawl inside him and revel in the bliss he was provoking but her spinning head and the need for oxygen forced her to break the kiss. Marco had certainly won this battle. She was putty in his hands.

"I like that look in your eye even more," he said between pants.

"Got them," Zander called from behind them. Whether he had seen the kiss and chose to ignore it or simply hadn't seen, she didn't know. He confidently pulled her from Marco's embrace and into his. He took her mouth in a thorough kiss then looked up at Marco. "You even hit a pothole and I'll kick your ass."

Symone could only lick her lips as Marco ushered her into her car. The mixture of Zander's flavor on her tongue mingled perfectly with the remnants of Marco's. It was the most potent aphrodisiac she'd ever encountered. The perfection of them was enough to cement her growing conviction that she would never be able to settle for one or the other. She wanted both.

Adrenaline pumped through her veins as Marco drove, if not completely burning off the alcohol at least lessening the effect of it. Her desires were *crystal clear*. She vibrated with anticipation and excitement as a plan formed in her head. She would entice them both into her bed if it was the last thing she did.

* * * *

The red tail lights flashed, and the left signal light blinked. Zander carefully watched every move the car in front of him made. There was one hell of a precious package in that vehicle. If there was any indication of Marco being less than perfect in his operation of the car, one wrong move and he was prepared to force the car to the shoulder and remove said precious package.

Symone was getting under his skin. If he were completely honest with himself, he'd admit that she had wormed her way into other deeper places too. He wasn't ready to admit it, though, he barely knew her. Throw in the fact that she was obviously attracted to another man and he'd be smart not to let her get any further than his skin. Unfortunately, that was not going to be an easy task. Symone intrigued him. From the way she looked to the workings of her mind. Everything about her just added a check mark on his list of what he was looking for in a woman. Not everything, he reminded himself. Marco sure as hell wasn't on that list.

When he'd first encountered Marco in Menjo's and seen him setting his sights on Symone he hadn't been too worried. Even after their shared breakfast, he still hadn't been concerned. He'd put Marco in the category of 'big, muscular and not very much substance'. A total beef head.

After hearing Symone talk about him and spending time with him today, he was feeling a little nervous. Oh, he had no doubt Marco was a player, he'd seen him before in some of the local clubs and had never seen the same girl on his arm more than once. The way he looked at Symone, though, he wasn't sure that she was just his newest conquest. He looked at her with a look that was hard to fake—one of real tenderness. He doubted Polo was going for an Academy Award any time soon. It was obvious he had a real affection for her. So where did that leave him?

Symone was another little equation he couldn't quite figure out. What was her objective? Sometimes she gave the impression that she was just out for a good time and thrilled with the attention they were showing her. Other times she would say something or give him a look that made him think *longing*. Then again, he could be completely out of his fucking mind and should stop trying to analyze everything the two of them said or did. He should just enjoy the ride, wherever it took him and for as long as it lasted. He should concentrate solely on the pleasure he could derive from it.

He had made it twenty-seven years without being in a committed relationship, why was he even considering it now? Many of his friends were married with children and he had witnessed the stress such choices added to life. Mortgages, increased health insurance costs, college tuition, sensible cars. Not that he had anything against anyone that wanted those things, but he was perfectly happy with his house on the beach, the Nissan 370z Nismo Edition sports car sitting in his driveway and variety in bed partners. He couldn't have enjoyed those little luxuries being married with two-point-five children.

That's exactly it. It's all about pleasure and living in the moment. Why the fuck am I even thinking about this shit?

He pulled into the driveway of a little bungalow behind Symone's car and knew he was talking smack. The way his stomach eased and how he let out the breath he had been holding said it all. All the pep talks and plans didn't mean dick. He was already in way over his head, already betting on winning this little contest between him and Marco.

The stakes were high, and he knew, without a shadow of a doubt, he wouldn't be throwing in his cards anytime soon.

Marco helped a laughing Symone out of the car. His stomach clenched again and his pulse increased as Marco took her into his arms and hugged her. At first, he thought it might be a twinge of jealousy causing his symptoms, but when Marco placed a kiss to her lips Zander's dick twitched. He wasn't just jealous, he was aroused as hell. He looked down at his treacherous dick. "What the fuck is your problem? Since when do we share?"

The response was another twitch as *share* passed his lips.

Symone waved a hand for him to join her and Marco. He adjusted the greedy bastard in his shorts, took a deep breath then stepped out of the car.

Chapter Seven

The look on Zander's face was unreadable as he approached, but as he stepped up and his gaze met hers there was no mistaking the desire that swam in those dark depths. He might be a little wary after seeing Marco take her into his arms, but as Symone let her eyes travel down his body to the thick bulge in the front of his shorts, it was clear he was also very turned on. That was an emotion she could deal with tonight.

She held out her hand to Marco. "Keys? You guys want to come in for a nightcap?"

Marco handed them to her and inquired, "What kind of nightcap are you offering?" He mimicked her gesture but rather than Zander's body, it was hers.

The slow exploration caused her hard nipples to stiffen further and press against the silk of her bikini top. Her skin prickled from his attention as he made his way down then back up to hold her gaze. What he hoped would be her answer to his question was clear. He wasn't counting on liquor or a cup of coffee.

"Guess you'll have to come in and find out," she said seductively as she moved toward the front door and beckoned them both with the crook of her finger. "Coming?"

"Close," Marco joked as he quickly fell in step behind her, Zander practically at his side.

She knew the feeling well. She'd been close most of the night. It wouldn't take much to push her over the edge. She let them into the house and dropped her keys on the small table next to the door. "I'm going to grab an ice coffee. Would either of you like one?"

"Water is fine for me." Marco made his way to the couch and took a seat.

Zander sat at the opposite end. "Yeah, same here."

Symone grabbed a couple of bottles of water and a can of mocha latte. "You know," she said as she handed them their drinks and took the chair across from them, "Todd wanted to know which one of you was my date. I'm pretty sure he was hoping he could get a crack at one of you."

Zander's eyes went wide as saucers and the bottle he was bringing to his lips hesitated for a second before he took a sip.

Marco gave her a sultry look, then glanced at Zander. "Oh really? Well he isn't as hot as Z here, but I think they would make a very cute couple." He looked back at her and winked.

Zander coughed and sputtered, nearly spitting out the water he'd just taken in. Symone laughed at the look of mischief in Marco's eyes and the red cheeks Zander was sporting. "You are so bad," she chastised Marco.

"Me? My intentions are honorable. I was just trying to hook him up with a date. Don't want Z here to be lonely."

Zander got himself under control and set the water bottle on the table. He turned to Marco. "Oh, I won't be lonely. No need for you to concern yourself over me." He turned back to Symone and waggled his eyebrows. "I got all the company I need right here, thank you very much."

"What about poor Todd? Aren't you concerned about him being lonely?" she giggled.

"Why don't you come over here so we can all discuss poor Todd's options?" Marco patted the couch between him and Zander.

"Good idea. Let's discuss Polo's date with Todd, seeing as he thinks he's so *adorable*."

Symone studied them over the rim of her coffee mug as she took a sip. Both men teased harmlessly, but the predatory look in their eyes told her they liked the idea of discussing it up close and personal even more. And she did mean up close and personal, since neither moved over to allow her more room between them. She'd be practically sitting on their laps if she gave in to the offer.

Okay, Miss Big Talk. Here's the chance to seduce these two gorgeous creatures into your bed.

For a moment, the apprehension started to win out over the excitement and arousal. This was what she wanted, wasn't it? To be the sole focus of both these men as they gave her unimaginable pleasure. Yet in the back of her mind, there was still that good girl screaming at her to take a breath and reconsider. This wasn't her. She was the kind who gave her heart too easily, believed in monogamy and Prince Charming.

Yeah, and where has that gotten you? A broken heart and wounded pride.

Symone's gaze ran over their expectant faces. The taste of them still lingered on her tongue and the press of their bodies against hers was seared into her memory. She set down her drink on the side table and stood.

What the hell.

It was time to live in the moment. Take what she wanted for a change, and emotions and hearts be damned. If the saying, *'only the good die young'*, was true she planned to live a very, very long time. She couldn't argue that it was something she hadn't known would happen, premeditation would be easy to prove if anyone found the large box of condoms she had hidden away in her nightstand. Was that the same as wishful thinking?

She made her way across the room and situated herself between Marco and Zander. She felt completely wanton as she placed a hand on each of their thighs. "So who is going to go make Todd a very happy man?" she teased, knowing full well Todd would not be sampling either of their delights. Oh, hell yes, she was very greedy.

"You should definitely send Polo." Zander turned her head with the tip of his finger. He took her mouth with gentle but demanding lips. The instant their tongues met, she felt the vibration of his moan against it, which raced through her entire body.

Marco nuzzled her neck as Zander deepened the kiss. Her own moan was involuntary as pleasure soared inside her. It was too big to contain and she didn't even try.

"I'm thinking you would be more Todd's type, Z." Marco's warm breath tickled her sensitive skin. "A hot, exotic treat."

Zander broke the kiss, leaving Symone gasping to catch her breath as he moved down to the other side of her neck. "Yes, but he looks like the kind who would prefer American delights."

Exotic, American, hell she wanted it all as they continued to assault her skin with tongues, teeth and lips. It was a smorgasbord of pleasure, and she was beyond ready to indulge and devour.

"Then again," Marco purred against her skin, "perhaps Symone should decide."

Zander took Marco's words for the challenge they were and worked his way down her neck, teeth scraping across her collarbone. She gasped when he hit a particularly sensitive spot, and he zeroed in on it, sucking vigorously.

Marco would not be outdone. He moved down the other side of her neck to the swell of her breasts. He pushed it further when the tip of his tongue flicked across her skin at the exact moment he pulled the hand she had clutched to his thigh and placed it to the swell of his arousal. Her fingers instinctively curled around the impressive shaft. Her touch pulled a deep groan from him.

Easing away from Symone, Zander took in Marco's position, his eyes going straight to her hand on Marco's cock. He licked his lips and turned to meet her gaze. A fire roared to life in the pit of her stomach as she took in the ravenous look in those dark eyes.

"Not without a complete inspection of both of her choices." His voice was husky with barely contained desire. He took her mouth in a fierce kiss at the same moment he moved her other hand to his equally hard cock.

They were taking their competition to a whole new level. Her gladiators from the first night no longer fought for valor or supremacy over the other. Instead, they joined forces to send her to euphoric bliss. The dual sensations didn't allow for conscious thought as her body overruled her mind. Her skin barely contained the fire surging through her veins. She could only whimper and moan as her body moved on the waves of sensation.

She didn't know when her bikini top had been removed but she was acutely aware of the mouths surrounding her hard nipples. Felt the warm, moist heat, scrape of teeth and flicks of tongues all the way to her soul. Marco and Zander moved in perfect sync as they each laid a hand on her sex. Her hips thrust in unison with the contractions of her cunt. Zander's impressive cock twitched against her palm and his hips took on the same sensual rhythm of her own movements. Marco was more aggressive and demanding. He humped hard against her hand in the same domineering pace as his mouth.

She didn't know from whom it came, but as a blunt fingertip skimmed across her clit, it was the push she needed. She was flying as an orgasm rocketed through her body. Her entire frame went bowstring tight as convulsion after convulsion wracked through her system. When the last of the contractions eased, Symone opened her eyes to two sets of glowing predatory gazes.

Holy fucking hell. He'd never seen anything so raw and carnal in his life.

Marco had plenty of experience with his sexuality, he was the believer in try anything once, and a second time if it was good…and a lot if it was real good. He'd had real good before. And yet, he couldn't ever remember being so beyond arousal that the throb in his cock was pushing past the pleasurable ache and careening straight into unequivocal agony.

When Symone had given herself over to the pleasure, it had been as if she'd become unearthly. Her ecstasy had become tangible in the air around them. The heavy gasps for air and the dazed look on Zander's face as he stared at her convinced Marco that Zander had experienced it too.

He damn sure couldn't hold out long.

Symone licked her lips, her smile just this side of pure devil. "So what's the next event in your competition?" It was the only motivation he needed.

Marco swept her up into his arms and threw her over his shoulder caveman style. "Next event is I'm going to blow your ever-lovin' mind. Which way to the bed?"

Symone giggled and pinched his ass, causing him to jerk. "That way."

He couldn't see which way she was indicating but he didn't need to. Zander was already moving to the door just off the living room and opened it without hesitation. Obviously, he wasn't the only one in a hurry. He stepped into a small bedroom and couldn't tell a damn thing about the décor, he simply didn't care. What drew his eye was the king-size bed and he headed to it.

"Hey, wait a minute," Zander protested. "Isn't there always a coin toss in a competition to see which side goes first?"

"Call it, Z." Marco eased Symone down to sit on the edge of the bed, and reached for the hem of her cover up. He pulled it off in one swift movement.

Zander called out, "Heads", which was followed by the distinctive sound of a coin being slapped onto the nightstand. "Heads. I go first."

He leered down at Symone's sexy as hell body, pulse racing. "We weren't flipping to see who goes first, you moron. We were flipping for position."

The only thing marring the perfection before him was the bottoms of her bikini, and he planned to rectify the offensive covering now. He hooked his thumbs into the top of her waistband and pulled them slowly down her hips, keeping his gaze directly on hers. "There is no way in hell am I waiting to sample this." He leaned in and spoke against Symone's lips, encouraging her to lie back. He pulled the material down her long legs and let it fall to the floor.

A sharp intake of breath from next to him about summed it up. Marco's heart literally skipped a beat, while the pulse in his cock kicked into overdrive. He'd studied and painted fine works of art. He'd been privileged to sketch some beautiful bodies in his day, male and female, but with Symone's tanned body laid out across the white eyelet lace covering the bed, she transcended what he'd previously thought was beautiful.

Symone leaned back on her elbows. Her amber hair framed her in thick waves of silk. Her dark pink nipples beckoned to him with each rapid rise and fall of her chest. Though she had positioned her legs in such a way as to deny him the full delights of her body, he could see enough to know that every inch of her was smooth and bare. His mouth watered in anticipation of exploring it. And still, the thing that stole his breath was the hunger and need in those gorgeous green eyes. He'd give his soul to sate that hunger.

"Well?" he forced out past his constricted throat.

"All of it," Zander replied, awe in his voice.

Marco stole a glance at him. The man was literally shaking in an attempt to restrain himself and it looked as if the effort was taking every store of willpower. He doubted Zander could even make a choice at this point.

"You called heads," he pointed out. He let his fingertip brush the inside of Symone's inner thigh and moved it slowly up her trembling leg toward her sex. "Head is what you get and I get this," he murmured as his finger ghosted across her clit.

"For the first round," Zander countered and began to undress.

Marco chuckled as Symone's green eyes went wide at Zander's insistence that there would be more than one round in this event. He pulled his T-shirt over his head and began to unbutton his shorts. "Scared?" he asked her gently.

Symone met his eyes and shook her head slightly. She cleared her throat. "Should I be?" she asked, her voice breathless.

He eased his zipper down, his engorged shaft pressing hard against his fingers, eager for release from the constricting material. "Only of dying from pleasure."

"Her or me?" Zander questioned.

Marco peeked at Zander. He had removed his shirt and was sliding his shorts down over his hips as he continued to stare at Symone with a stunned look on his face. Marco wasn't sure if the look was for the sight before him, or the fact that he was even in this position or both. Marco had no desire to find out which at the moment. His cock jerked hard, giving him a little reminder that it wouldn't be denied. He removed a condom from his pocket before he shoved his shorts down and off.

Ribbons of arousal wound around him so tightly that the only thing he could concentrate on was finding his release. As he sheathed his engorged shaft, he encouraged Symone to roll over and positioned her on her hands and knees. He was barely conscious of Zander moving around the bed, couldn't comprehend what either was saying. He could only feel as he slid a finger into her tight, wet heat. As she pushed back and impaled herself on his invading finger with a loud gasp of pleasure, he added a second.

"Oh God, that feels good," Symone panted.

His dick seeped a steady stream in anticipation of being engulfed inside her tight sex. The sounds of passion, deep moans and harsh breaths coming from Zander and Symone drove him on. He positioned himself behind Symone, rubbed his cock against the silky softness of her ass, while he continued to thrust his fingers in and out of her clenching channel. She gave a muffled whimper when he pulled his fingers free. With a trembling hand, he guided his cock to the opening of her passage. He met Zander's gaze and knew the moment Symone took him deep into her throat. Zander's eyes rolled back in his head as he gave into his bliss.

Marco pushed farther into that perfect heat. He wanted to savor each and every inch slowly but Symone, wild with need, thrust back, taking him in to the hilt in one hard movement.

"Fuck!" he roared as her channel gripped his cock in a tight vice and severed the last thread he had on his control. He grabbed her hips in a bruising grasp and gave himself over completely to the ecstasy. He pounded into her, hips jerking, captivated by the sight of Zander's hard muscles working as he thrust in and out of her mouth.

A constant stream of curses and praises, mixed with pleas for *more* and *harder*, tumbled from Zander only heightened his own pleasure. Marco was beyond speech, reduced to a series of primal grunts as his sac drew up tight against his body and his cock swelled even further as his release threatened.

Gritting his teeth, he fought to hold his orgasm at bay, his entire body quaking with the effort. When Zander threw his head back, the thick cords of tendons bulged in his neck as he roared his release.

The sight demanded Marco's orgasm, and he was completely powerless against the force of it.

Chapter Eight

Warmth and contentment surrounded Symone. She snuggled in deeper as visions of Marco and Zander pleasuring her body, sending it to heights she didn't even know existed, flashed behind her closed lids.

It had been one hell of an erotic, very vivid dream. It had to be a dream because she was sure pleasures such as those she had experienced could only exist in fantasy. Reality was never that good. No way would she ever be so wanton and naughty in real life. Little Miss Prim and Proper, with a history of three steady boyfriends and not a single one-night stand on her list of accomplishments. Yeah, it had been one hell of a dream.

From the glow behind her closed lids, she could tell it was morning but some of her systems weren't back online yet. Not that she was ready for them to be. Floating in warm bliss was a rather nice way to wake up.

Unfortunately, her bladder had other ideas and made it painfully obvious that she wasn't going to enjoy the comfort for very much longer. Groaning, she tried to roll to the side of the bed when she connected with something solid. Her eyes snapped open and she found herself staring at the smooth golden skin of someone's back.

Not just anyone either. She recognized the wheat-blond hair and the broad shape and didn't need to see his face to know it was Marco. She snuck a glance over her shoulder, and sure enough, there was Zander's sleeping form. *Oh, my fucking God, it was real!*

Symone could only blink dumbly as the events of the night before came rushing back in all their explicit glory. Marco taking her from behind while she'd feasted on Zander's thick shaft, the way they'd moved and coaxed her before they'd switched positions and taken her again. She flopped back onto the bed as each wonderful detail came back to her.

Just the thought of it was enough for her heart to speed up and her inner walls to contract. *Ow!* Okay that wasn't such a good idea. From the twinge of pain between her legs, she had all the proof she needed that it actually had been reality.

Wow! If that's what it's like to be a bad girl, sign me up. What dumb-ass wants to be good when they could have pure naughty heaven right here on earth? I'm never going to be a good girl again!

She praised her decision to go with a bed frame without a footboard, scooted down beneath the cover and snuck out the end. Sliding against the covers caused static electricity in her hair and she tried smoothing it down, only to encounter a mass of snarls and tangles. Hair the length of hers did not do well overnight without being braided. It also hadn't helped that both men had been enthralled by her hair, oftentimes tugging it or running it through their fingers absentmindedly as their attentions were focused on other parts of her body. It had knotted and pressed against her sweat-soaked body before she'd fallen into a deep sleep. She could only imagine what it looked like now. No way did she want them to see her in her current condition, nor did she want to face them with dry morning mouth or red puffy eyes. One did not confront gods like these men without being at one's best.

She stood at the end of the bed and looked her fill as they slept. The space she had exited beckoned her but she resisted. *I could get used to this.*

Waking between the two of them was wonderful. She couldn't remember the last time she'd felt such warmth.

Don't even think about it. The reason it was so hot was because no emotions were involved. Don't ruin it now.

She chastised her stupidity and turned away. Without turning on the light, she eased into the bathroom and shut the door. She turned on the taps of the shower and once the water warmed to the right temperature, she stepped in.

Standing under the spray, Symone groaned as the jet of hot water pounded against her sore muscles, easing her as she contemplated what the little voice in her head was screaming at her. Never had anything she'd experienced been as phenomenal as the experience she'd had with Marco and Zander. Was it because there were no emotions involved? Was that what had made it so good? As she shampooed and conditioned her hair, she let that thought sink in.

It made sense. The only people she'd ever had sex with were men she'd thought she was in love with. Maybe not love, since she could now admit that she probably still didn't understand what love was, but at least men she had some emotional ties with on some level. Sure Marco and Zander had given and taken pleasure from her, but she was sating a physical need too. She had taken something that had been denied her for too long and she hadn't thought about how they were going to look at her in the morning, hadn't cared what they thought about her as a person. It had been freeing to just give over to the sensations of her body without the restraints her heart put on it.

Her mind made up, she stepped out of the shower and dried quickly. If they woke up before she could get dressed, she would be a considerate host, smile and thank them for the evening and steer them to the door. If she were really lucky, she would finish dressing, grab her keys then head down to the local coffee shop for her morning dose of caffeine. She'd leave them a thank-you note and ask them to lock up behind themselves when they left. She really didn't know either of them that well but didn't think they would steal anything. Hell, she didn't really have anything worth stealing anyway, and if they did? It would be easier to replace the item than having to deal with the weird, awkward morning-after conversation.

Luck was on her side as she slipped into a pair of shorts and T-shirt. Neither man stirred while she scribbled a quick note and left it on the kitchen counter. She slid her feet into flip-flops, grabbed her keys then headed out of the door.

Pulling out of the drive, the real Symone made her way to the surface as guilt flooded her for being a coward. As her chest tightened around her heart, the new bad girl quickly jerked her away from those thoughts.

* * * *

The fact that he'd woken up alone next to Marco had been unexpected, but after relieving himself, Zander gathered up his scattered clothing and wandered out into the kitchen. The ache in his heart after reading Symone's note was even more unexpected.

The curt *'Thank you and lock up behind yourselves when you leave'* seemed completely out of character from what he knew of Symone. Not that he knew her all that well but from their phone conversations and the way she'd interacted with others at the party he knew what a sweet and caring person she was.

Maybe she had run because he'd gotten carried away last night? He always tried to be a thoughtful lover, tried to give as much pleasure as he received and never once had he been accused of being selfish. Yet, Symone had managed to obliterate any restraint he'd thought he had. He'd been so consumed by the out-of-this-world pleasure that he couldn't swear to the fact that he'd made sure she had reached it with him.

Guilt assaulted Zander and he felt it as a sick feeling in his gut.

Fuck, Symone, what the hell did you do to me?

He hadn't been drunk or incapacitated in anyway and still he could barely remember anything past watching Symone shudder as her first orgasm had ripped through her body when they'd still been on the couch. Much of what had transpired once they'd reached her bed was a blur of one shattering climax

after another. It was raw animalistic desire at its
deepest level, and he'd been completely uncivilized
giving himself over to it completely.

He found his keys by the door and noticed Marco's
shoes still sitting on the floor. *Fuck!* Marco had driven
Symone's car and his was still back at Sedesa's. If he
didn't drive him back to get his car, Marco would have
the perfect opportunity to still be here when Symone
returned. Like that was going to happen. He turned
and headed back to the bedroom.

Marco was still in the same position he'd been in
when Zander had gotten out of bed, his big frame still
wrapped around a pillow. He took in his naked torso
and got another unexpected shock of electricity. His
dick twitched and began to fill as he took in the thick
muscles and smooth skin.

What the hell?

He'd never been attracted to another man. Sure, he
could admit when a guy was attractive like Gerard
Butler or Johnny Depp but they didn't make his dick
perk up and take notice. Panic shot through his system.

*Breathe, man. It's okay. There has to be a reasonable
explanation for this.*

He ripped his gaze from Marco and tried to
concentrate. Last night he had experienced something
beyond the norm, bliss on a whole new level and Marco
had been there. It had been his first experience in
sharing a woman with anyone so maybe that was it. His
stomach began to ease and he sighed in relief with the
thought. That had to be it. It was the fact that he now
associated Marco with the pleasure he'd had with
Symone, and Marco just happened to be a part of it. *But
what if…?*

Nope, he wasn't even going there.

Waking Marco and having to deal with him was the last thing he wanted to do, especially with the real fear that his dick might get all stupid in front of Marco and he'd have to explain why. Then again, there was no way in hell he was going to leave the man in Symone's bed either. With one last steadying breath, he reached out and shoved at Marco's shoulder. To say he was relieved that he didn't feel a jolt of lust when he touched the man was the understatement of the year. "Hey, Polo, time to get up."

Marco grumbled and rolled away, still clutching the pillow.

He shoved at him again. "Rise and shine."

"Go away," Marco grumbled, without moving or opening his eyes.

I don't think so.

"Don't make me jerk your ass out of that bed," he threatened.

Zander ducked just in time to miss the pillow that was aimed at his head.

"I'm sleeping. Don't you have some animals to feed? Cages to clean?"

"No, I have your sorry ass to drive to your car. So get up."

Marco muttered something Zander couldn't make out. He was sure it was something colorful given the furrowed brow and nasty glare Marco shot at him as he sat up. He didn't care as long as the man was up and moving.

Marco rubbed at his eyes. "Where's Symone?"

"Gone," Zander answered firmly.

"What the hell do you mean gone?" He grunted unhappily and threw back the covers.

"Gone. You know not here, left."

Marco narrowed his eyes at Zander. "What the fuck did you do?" he demanded angrily.

Zander had to turn away as Marco stood, without even trying to cover himself. He wasn't about to test his theory that it was Marco's involvement with him and Symone that had caused a reaction earlier. He spotted his quarter on the bedside table and nabbed it. He stuffed it into the pocket of his shorts, sure it wouldn't send the right message if he left it behind. *Oh look, a tip.* He shook his head and turned to let Marco dress.

"I asked you what the hell you did?" Marco asked again, clearly annoyed as he followed Zander out into the living room, while slipping on his shorts.

"Why do you think I did anything?" he countered.

"Um, let's see. I'm sleeping, you're awake, and she's gone? You tell me?" His sarcasm was thick as he gathered up the rest of his clothes and finished dressing.

"Maybe you fart in your sleep or snore, ever fucking think of that? Who knows? I woke up and she was gone. Nice note in the kitchen for you, though."

Marco stomped into the kitchen and snatched the note from the counter. His scowl intensified as he read it. "What the hell is this?"

It's a dismissal, you beef-head. "It's called a note. You know, something you write on paper with a writing instrument." He studied Marco for a moment. "You do know how to read, don't you?" He headed for the door. He wanted a shower, coffee and more sleep. Not necessarily in that order.

"Fuck off, Z. I had one hell of a time last night and the way Symone was moaning and screaming, I know she did too." Marco's eyes wandered down Zander's body before traveling back up to meet his eyes. He licked his lips. "From the looks of it you were having one hell of a good time too, so why the dismissal?"

Zander refused to acknowledge the obvious taunt — flat out forbade his body to respond to the way Marco looked at him.

"How the hell am I supposed to understand what a woman does? You're the expert here." He opened the front door and stepped out, leaving it ajar to give Marco no choice but to follow.

"Expert," Marco laughed as he followed Zander to the car. He walked over to the passenger side and leaned on the roof as Zander unlocked his door. "Were you checking out my technique last night, Z?"

Zander frowned, trying think back on the night before. Had he been checking Marco out? Damn if he could remember what he'd done, most of it was still hazy. He opened his door and got in. "Is that what they call it these days?" he asked as he reached over and unlocked the other door.

"You were! Damn, I'm flattered." Marco snorted as he eased in next to him.

"Did you lock her door behind you?" He ignored the statement, choosing to change the subject to one he was more comfortable with. He had some questions of his own he wanted answered but now was not the time to be doing it, especially with the shit-eating grin on Marco's face as he batted his lashes as him. Zander started the car and backed out of the drive.

"Yeah, I locked it. Why? Did you want to go for one last..."

"If you finish that sentence, I swear to God, I will throw you out of this fucking car and run over you." He threw the car into gear and stomped on the gas. "Twice."

Marco threw his head back and laughed.

The sooner he got this cocky bastard out of his car the better. He was just going to have to step up his competitive skills. The sooner he won Symone over, the quicker he could get rid of this irritating little shit. He glanced at Marco from the corner of his eye.

Okay, irritating sexy shit.

Chapter Nine

A plate of seafood pasta salad was set down in front of Symone, making her stomach rumble. She thanked the waiter and dove in.

The current multiple sales she was working on was kicking her butt and she barely found time to eat, let alone sit down while doing it. The only good thing to come out of the hectic pace she'd been racing at was that she hadn't had a chance to sit and think about Marco and Zander.

That wasn't entirely true, since she found herself thinking about them with a healthy dose of guilt often enough. At least her heavy workload offered a distraction from dwelling on it.

Both had called her the morning she'd snuck out of her house like a coward, and needless to say neither of them had been happy about her going AWOL. She didn't understand how people could play the role of *player*. Sure, the sex had been beyond her wildest expectations but the guilt was a bitch to live with. How the hell did people do it over and over? How did they leave the emotions out of it and just enjoy the physical aspects of the encounter?

She was finding out, for her personally, that there was no such thing as unemotional sex. She wasn't in love with either of them. Those emotions or anything remotely associated with that were firmly tucked behind a closed and deadbolt locked heart. Guilt, however, was one emotion she had plenty of.

It was the reason she had agreed to see them both again, that and the fact that she generally liked being in their company. It also scared the hell out of her. They were both the kind of men she could see herself falling for if she wasn't careful. From past experience, that was a very bad thing. Opening up her heart wasn't something she was ready for.

So much for your determination to become a bad girl.

Bad girl didn't mean she couldn't still have a heart. The tricky part was *playing* the bad girl and not losing said heart. It might be a frightening thought, but she could easily admit that the idea of spending another evening in bliss with Marco and Zander might be worth any risk.

She finished her salad, washed it down with her water with lemon then paid the bill. If she sat too long she would more than likely try to talk herself out of what she was about to do. Spending the afternoon on a private beach with two gods such as Marco and Zander was like gambling in a high-stakes game, but instead of money on the table, it was her heart. However, the chance at a jackpot in the form of spending another night in their arms again made the risks seem pretty insignificant at the moment. Then again, she was sure many people in Gamblers Anonymous had thought the same thing before they'd hit rock bottom.

Any hopes of sitting in her car and take a few moments to calm her racing heart died when she pulled into Zander's driveway later that day and found him standing on the front porch.

The way he looked, she needed those calming moments even more now. He stood, leaning against the rail of the porch, dressed in tan cargo shorts and a white tank top. The light colors highlighted his dark olive skin to perfection. The material of his shirt stretched tightly against his defined torso, accentuated each ridge and valley of that sculpted belly. Symone's heart sped to double time as she turned off the car. The smile on his face set off an internal chain reaction that left her breathless and her panties damp.

Use it to your advantage, girl. You're a bad girl. Focus on the pleasure. With one last deep breath, she grabbed her bag and stepped out.

"Good to see you didn't have any trouble finding me," Zander called as he waved. "Most people end up calling and I have to navigate them in."

She could understand that. There had been so many turns and winding roads, that it was a stretch to call some of them roads, more like trails. Thank God for her GPS. She held up her cell phone as she shut the car door. "Gotta love modern technology."

Zander met her halfway up the walk and wrapped her in a tight embrace. "I'm so glad you could come." He nuzzled her neck.

That internal detonation grew at the first contact of his lips against her skin.

"Mmm, you look amazing. It's so good to see you again."

Oh yeah, it was good to see him, even better to feel him against her. She felt desire race down her spine. "It's good to see you too." She pulled back a little before she ran the risk of losing herself in him right here on the front lawn. "Your place is beautiful."

Zander gave her a little pout but released her and took her hand, leading her to the front door. "Thanks. I love it out here. It's like owning my own little private piece of the universe. The closest neighbor is five miles away." He opened the door and ushered her in.

From the outside, the house appeared to be small, but in this case, looks were totally deceiving. As she entered, she realized that the house, with its wide-open floor plan, was extremely large. The entire western side of the house was made of glass with an impressive deck attached. The view of the small beach and the gulf beyond was stunning. She would bet that Zander had seen some amazing sunsets with a view like that.

"Wow, this isn't just beautiful, you have your own little paradise on earth."

"Now you know why I don't mind not having any neighbors. Can I get you anything to drink?"

"Water is fine."

The inside of the house was masculine, decorated in dark, oversized leather furniture arranged to enjoy either the view beyond the windows or the large plasma TV mounted to the wall. He'd accentuated everything in muted shades of red, orange and yellows. All the colors she was sure he had seen in the setting sun. It was impressive but couldn't hold her attention with the view beckoning her. "Do you mind if I check out the deck?"

"Not at all. I'll meet you out there with our drinks."

Symone set her bag down near the couch and headed out to the deck. The salty ocean breeze and the sounds of gulls over the rush of the tide were a symphony to the senses. It literally stole her breath away. She clutched the railing and tried to take in every minute detail of the majestic scene.

The beauty of her surroundings intensified as Zander moved up behind her. His heat engulfed her as completely as the afternoon sun. He handed her a bottle of water, which she graciously took with trembling fingers and swallowed a few sips. The cool liquid soothed her constricted throat. He was melting her with just his nearness, something she could not afford to let happen.

"I thought Marco was meeting us here?"

Zander stiffened slightly as his free hand moved around her waist and rested it against her stomach as he pulled her closer. "I'm hoping he got lost."

As he began to place soft kisses against her temple, she realized how bad an idea it would be to spend the afternoon alone with him. Marco and Zander were easier to relegate to the 'just sex' category. If she spent alone time with either of them it would be too easy to forget the why of it. "Marco doesn't strike me as the kind of person who would let getting lost slow him down."

"You picked up on that too, huh?" Zander chuckled. "He's pretty determined, I'll give him that."

Symone turned in his arms and looked up at him. "And what about you? Are you as determined when you want something?"

He held her gaze for a long moment. Desire and confidence swirled together in the depths of his brown eyes. The intensity caused her to shudder.

Zander didn't answer. He leaned down and placed his lips against hers. His tongue tickled her bottom lip as he encouraged her to open to him. Symone greedily allowed him into her mouth and savored his flavor. His soft moan vibrated against her tongue and sent a wave of lust flowing through her.

Instinctively she grabbed the back of his head, tightened her fingers in the thick strands, and deepened the kiss. The way Zander responded, took control of the kiss, left her dazed and proved just how determined he could be without saying a word.

The world around her disappeared as she gave in to the kiss. Everything about him—his flavor, scent and the caress of his body against hers demanded undivided attention. The soft silk of her sundress was a poor defense against the full impact of his body. His hard shaft pressed against her stomach as he slowly began to rock against her in a sensual rhythm. Her own body responded without permission and she couldn't control the need to follow his lead. She rubbed against him wantonly as he feasted on her mouth with such ferocity that she was powerless against it.

As the movements of their bodies intensified, she stopped caring about anything except how good she felt. How good he felt against her. Zander broke the kiss, leaving her panting and breathless. He kissed his way along her cheek until his harsh breath warmed the skin beneath her ear. "I have to…"

Whatever he was about to say was cut off by a loud pounding on the front door, followed by the shrill sound of a doorbell. "I really do hate that man." Zander grunted as he pulled away.

As she watched Zander turn and stomp off toward the front door, she had to steady herself on the railing of the deck. Her legs felt like they were made of rubber, barely capable of holding her upright.

At that very moment, as her sex contracted and her heart rate continued to beat out a rapid pace, she could admit that Marco wasn't her favorite person in the world either. Not him as a person, but his timing sure sucked.

* * * *

Fuck! He hated being late. Today was the worst possible time for it to happen. It gave the Zoo-man more time alone with Symone than he was comfortable with. He wouldn't put it past that little fucker to move right in and seduce Symone behind his back.

Hell, if he had the chance he'd have done it himself, and he was just pissed that the roles weren't reversed. The sad thing was he had no one to blame other than himself. He'd spent more time in the shower and in front of the mirror than he normally did when getting ready to go out. Well, the extra time in the shower had been necessary.

Just the idea of seeing Symone again had him rock hard and his balls drawing up tight. He'd had to relieve a little pressure or he'd have been in real danger of popping a nut the moment he laid eyes on her. Even with that delay, he would have made it on time if Joe hadn't decided to hire a new guy today of all days to do the detail work. Marco didn't trust anyone with his baby except Joe's Garage. He and his buddy, Dean, had spent the last two years painstakingly restoring every inch of his 1970 Monte Carlo. Just like his personal appearance, he'd wanted her to shine today too. Oh, and was she ever sweet. He loved that freshly bathed scent. He just hadn't expected it to take a half hour longer than usual.

He'd had to backtrack once but he'd found Zander's house without too much trouble. He'd pulled into the driveway and had to envy the seclusion Z had. His own condo was nice but not very private. Neighbors came and went at all hours of the day and night and he'd made the huge mistake of wanting his condo to overlook the pool. Now he listened to kids screaming, splashing and laughing all day and half the night.

Stepping out of the car and taking in the landscape, that hadn't been the only thing he was envious about. Symone's blue Ford Focus sat in the drive. He glanced down at his watch. If she had been on time, Z had probably had a full twenty minutes alone with her, and dammit, that hot son of a bitch could probably get her out of her panties in ten.

Impatiently, he'd pounded on the door and rung the doorbell at the same time.

He was just getting ready to pound harder when he spotted Zander through the glass panes moving to the door. A deep frown on his face informed Marco that Zander had either been hoping Marco wouldn't show up, would be late. Or maybe he'd interrupted something. Marco couldn't help but glance down Z's body when he flung open the door and noticed the front of Z's shorts was tented. Yup, he'd interrupted them. Good!

"Hey, Zoo-man, sweet crib," he complimented as he stepped in. Not that he was really looking at the décor. He was too busy scanning the area for what he wanted to feast his eyes on most. He spotted Symone on the back deck and felt pulled toward her.

"Why don't you just come on in and make yourself at home," Zander said sarcastically.

"Don't mind if I do. Whatcha got cold to drink?" he asked over his shoulder as he still moved toward Symone. "I'll have a beer if you got it."

Zander muttered something but Marco wasn't paying attention. He was moving out of the door as he narrowed in on his target, and in two long strides across the deck, he swept Symone up in his arms. "Damn, girl, you look good enough to eat."

Symone laughed that small sound that sent a tingle right to the center of his chest. "Wow, quite the greeting. You'd have thought you missed me or something."

"Hell yeah, I missed you," he said with certainty as he placed a kiss on her temple. Her sweet scent, reminding him of wild flowers, sent another tingle to him but slightly lower than his chest.

"It's only been a few days." She swatted him playfully. "Put me down."

He held her tight, refusing her request. "Only if you give me a kiss."

She smiled and looked up at him from under those long curling lashes. "Plant one on me," she drawled.

He didn't need a second invitation. He took her mouth and kissed her thoroughly, not pulling away until they were both breathing hard. Zander cleared his throat behind them, and Marco reluctantly set Symone back on her feet and released her.

"Your timing sucks, Z-Man," he complained as he turned and took the beer Zander held out to him.

"Yeah, no worse than yours," he muttered.

Damn good thing too.

If that little shit at the garage had been just ten minutes slower, he didn't doubt he'd have interrupted a hell of a lot more than a kiss. The way Z had been sporting wood when he'd answered the door, he could just bet they hadn't been playing checkers.

He couldn't resist glancing down to see if the bulge was still on display. He caught a glimpse of it before Zander moved past, and damn if Marco's eyes didn't narrow in on his tight ass. He'd had a lot of opportunity to think about Symone and the pleasures of her body over the last few days and he'd also found himself thinking about Zander.

Not that he was ready to admit it to the man. The few jokes he'd thrown out had already stunned him, and Marco was still contemplating how he could work Zander's apparent homophobia against him. The actual internal battle he was dealing with was more of whether he should try to use it to his advantage to get Zander to back off or use it to attract the man.

He'd always loved to experiment with different kinks. How the hell could something be dismissed if it wasn't tried, right? He'd been with two women at the same time in the past, but had never had the opportunity to share a bed with just a man and a woman. There had been that one time while he'd been in Tampa but the couple hadn't done anything for him and he'd turned them down. It excited the fuck out of him now, even more than the thought of having two women.

Probably the unknown of it heightened his excitement, and if he were being honest, he'd always been a little curious to find out what the big deal was about same-gender sex. The couple of man-on-man porns he'd watched, while hot, just hadn't been that great. Oh, he'd gotten off, with a little help from his hand and some lube, but the twinks on the screen really hadn't done it for him.

Until now he hadn't really felt a strong enough desire to actually want to cross that line, but looking at Zander as he wrapped an arm around Symone and whispered in her ear, the desire was suddenly very strong. He gave himself an internal shake.

One conquest at a time, my man.

First up? Owning Symone, then he'd give more thought to setting his sights on seducing Zander, but that didn't mean he had any intentions of ignoring the man.

He moved to Symone's other side and wrapped an arm around her waist. "So what's on the agenda for the day?"

Chapter Ten

The sun was halfway through its descent, and the heat of the day was beginning to recede to a more bearable temperature.

Symone reclined against Zander, his hard body radiating the warmth it had captured from the setting sun against her side. They'd played in the surf, Zander and Marco showing off doing their impersonations of Muscle Beach until her sides had ached from laughter.

Though they still seemed to be in competition mode, the playfulness they had developed at Sedesa's party had returned and she could see their relationship changing. Sure, they were still trying to win her over, but the two of them were becoming fast friends even without her around, which was a very good thing in her way of thinking.

She doubted she would be around in the future, but perhaps they would have a lasting friendship. She was sure neither of them would admit it if asked, but she knew it. The way they laughed easily with each other.

Even the scowls they tried to give one another held fondness and were less harsh.

Symone understood what they saw in the other. The way she was beginning to think of them was changing as the day wore on. They were becoming personalities and people, rather than something to slake her sexual appetite. It was a very dangerous way to think of them, and it was becoming harder and harder to convince herself that it was all about sex and nothing more. It was getting to be the time she moved on. The one night of meaningless, mind-numbing sex she wanted had been amazing and it should have stopped there. It had been stupid to accept their invite today.

Well, maybe not. If I'm lucky I'll get to enjoy another round of incredible sex with them and then end it.

She ignored the little twist in her gut at the thought of never seeing them again but pushed it away. The little twist was gravy compared to a heart stomped on. Yup, she was living in this moment and nothing more.

Zander's fingertips brushed along her side and caused her to squirm away from the tickling sensation.

"No moving," Marco chastised before returning his concentration once again to the sketch he was working on.

"It's not my fault. He keeps tickling me."

"I'm bored. How much longer are you going to be, Polo?" He leered down at Symone. "And I'm hungry."

The look in his eyes made her shudder. At that moment, his stomach growled loudly. "For food too," he chuckled.

"A couple more minutes. Haven't the two of you ever been told that patience is a virtue?"

"Aww, Marco," she cooed. "Are you worried about protecting my virtue? How sweet."

Zander snorted. "I doubt Polo could protect anyone's virtue. Shatter it, maybe, but protect it? Not a chance."

"Jealous, Z?" Marco inquired without looking up. Even with his head bowed, he couldn't hide the smile. "Or are you worried about me shattering yours as well?"

Symone's sex clenched at the sultry lilt to Marco's voice. She wasn't sure if Marco was being serious or just trying to bait Zander but obviously her body liked the idea. It liked it a whole lot.

"You son of a bitch," Zander grumbled. "I bet you haven't even drawn a damn thing. Probably just your sick excuse for ogling me."

"Maybe," his reply was soft and teasing.

Zander jumped to his feet and went after him.

"Hey, I told you not to move." He closed his sketchbook and jerked it out of Zander's reach just before his hands closed around it. He got to his feet and started to back away.

"Don't make me beat you," Zander threatened as he slowly advanced on Marco.

"Symone, call him off. He wants to beat me." He waggled his brows at Zander. "Or is that beat me off? Mmm, come on, you sexy thing. Beat me."

Symone had just enough time to scurry over and rescue the sketchbook before the two of them began wrestling. As their play became more physical, she couldn't pull her eyes away. As they continued to struggle, their sweat-slicked bodies slid together, and their grunts and panting breaths took on a sexual tone. At least for Symone they did.

When Marco draped his larger body over Zander's back in an attempt to pin him, it was like a lightning strike directly to her core. Jesus, all that raw power coming together in ecstasy instead of a display of strength had her breath coming in short pants as her system flooded with arousal. She doubted she would ever voice her naughty thoughts aloud, but holy hell she could dream. She couldn't think of anything hotter than watching these two powerful men joined together.

Well, maybe being part of it would be hotter, but either way she would give anything to experience it. Her thoughts took on a vivid picture in her head. No longer did she see the two men wrestling and laughing. They tangled together, their heads thrown back in bliss, as they lost themselves to orgasmic pleasure. As the fantasy in her head played out, her body began to tremble from the potent aphrodisiac.

She was vibrating with lust, the walls of her sex seeping with each contraction. She jerked, nearly falling when Marco placed a hand at the small of her back.

"Earth to Symone." He snapped a finger in front of her face. "Anyone home?"

She forced the lust down enough to blink and answer him. "Uh…Yeah, I think I may have had too much sun," she lied. She had definitely had too much heat that had left her dizzy but it had nothing to do with the sun.

Zander and Marco gave each other a quizzical look. Marco shrugged. "How about we head up and see about some grub?"

"Sounds like a plan to me," Zander agreed, as he gathered up the blankets and cooler. "And a shower. I have sand in places that it has no business being thanks to this Neanderthal."

"You're welcome," Marco snorted.

Great! Now the image of them wrapped together in the shower as water cascaded down their bodies popped into her head and sent another punch directly to her center. She silently groaned as she followed them back to the house. If she didn't get her shit together and get a little control over her libido...

Who was she kidding? There was no way of getting it under control with the two of them around. The best she could hope for was to have it completely sated before she had to make the long trek back home.

Zander used the excuse of having to shake out the blankets to get a moment alone. He waited until Symone and Marco had gone into the house before he pulled the blanket from his body. The way his dick was straining against the material of his shorts wasn't something he had wanted on display, not after he'd been wrestling with Marco anyway. Had it been Symone, he'd have displayed it proudly. It just pissed him off to no end the way his traitorous body responded to the irritating man. He walked to the railing of the deck and began to shake the sand from the blankets.

What the hell was happening to him? He just couldn't understand why he had such a strong physical reaction to what he viewed as his competition. Technically, he'd been half hard from Symone being curled up against his side. So maybe that was why he had reacted the way he had.

That's got to be it. I'm not attracted to men.
Never have been, never will be.

Relief filled him, allowing him to take a full breath as he accepted the excuse his disbelieving mind was throwing at him. It was simply a reaction to the strenuous physical exertion after Symone had been so near. It had to be, it had started with her.

His body just hadn't made the switch over from female to male quick enough. He glanced down at his still-tented shorts. "Some days I really hate you," he muttered as he draped the blanket over the lounge chair. He thumped the fickle bastard, wincing in pain as he walked into the house to join Symone and Marco.

"So what does everyone..." He stopped dead in his tracks, the words dying in his throat.

Marco had Symone in his arms, and from the way he was devouring her mouth, he didn't have to finish the sentence, he knew exactly what Marco wanted to eat. They either hadn't heard him come in or had chosen to ignore him. Neither of which he was going to tolerate. He might be feeling a little freaked out by the earlier events but he had no doubts that he wanted Symone.

No way in hell was he going to cower from Marco's innuendos and hand Symone to him without a fight.

He moved up behind Symone and pressed his body against hers as his lips sought out the warm skin of her neck. She shuddered against him and the pulse at her neck increased. He sucked the delicate skin into his mouth, groaning at the flavor and the way it vibrated against his tongue. He was careful with his hands. He didn't want to take the chance of coming in contact with Marco's skin. The last thing he wanted was another unwanted sensation caused by the man. He kneaded Symone's shoulders as he continued his assault on her neck.

"Hey, this is my dinner," Marco lightly scolded.

Zander lifted his eyes without breaking the contact with Symone's skin and met Marco's gaze. The mischief and hunger obvious in Marco's nearly black eyes caused his breath to catch. *Goddammit.* His dick wasn't the only one he hated at the moment.

Marco and his fucking constant taunts and husky voice were pushing him to the edge of insanity. So many emotions warred in him that he wasn't sure whether he should punch Marco in his too damn sexy face or kiss him.

Where the fuck did that come from?

Symone pushed her luscious ass against his throbbing shaft, and the soft pants of her breath brought all his focus back to her. She was what he wanted at this moment, not trying to figure out what the fuck was wrong with his head.

"My house, my dinner rules," he drawled. He took the opportunity Marco had presented him with by easing his grip on Symone, and spun her around in his arms.

She gasped as he pulled her hard against him, but he didn't give her or Marco a chance to protest before he took her mouth in a deep, thorough kiss. All the irritation, anger and confusion he was feeling morphed into passion as her flavor burst across his taste buds. He probed and prodded with his tongue, seeking out more of the delicious flavor until he'd explored every inch of her mouth and still he wanted more.

"Greedy bastard," Marco grumbled.

Zander ignored him.

As he sucked at Symone's tongue, he explored the fleshy mounds of her ass with his hand. All thoughts of Marco and the reaction he had to him were forgotten. His need, his only desire was to bury himself in the warm depths of Symone and stay there. When his oxygen-deprived lungs begged for air he did release her mouth. He laid his forehead against hers and breathed in her gasping breath, taking it deep inside him. "Very greedy for you," he whispered for Symone's ears only. Or so he thought.

"Greed is one of the seven deadly sins, Zoo-man." Marco tugged at Symone, but Zander refused to release her.

Still resting his head against Symone, he watched the swirls of gold float in her green eyes. "What a way to go."

"No one is having me for dinner until I get a shower." Symone giggled softly. "Sand is not conducive to soft caresses," she teased.

Oh yeah. Symone in the shower, naked and slick? That was a delight he would relish.

Marco forced his arm between their bodies and lifted Symone off her feet. Zander either had to release his grip or risk doing harm to her. He allowed Marco to take her from his arms and glared at him. "You're going to find your ass booted out the front door if you keep your shit up."

"There he goes about my ass again," Marco chuckled and started to move toward the bathroom. "Symone, will you watch my ass while we're in the shower and keep the animal man off it?"

"How do you know I don't want him to get your ass?" Symone retorted.

Zander stopped dead in his tracks. He hoped she was joking. He shook off the uneasy feeling and followed Marco into the bathroom. Maybe it was his own ass he'd better keep an eye on.

He tried holding back the laughter when Zander froze at his tease. It was hopeless and he buried his face in Symone's neck to muffle it. He was only joking, mostly. Marco had given some thought to—okay, so he'd given a lot of thought to Zander, but it wasn't like he was going to act on any of the crazy impulses that were popping into his head at the moment. Right now, his focus was on Symone as he carried her to the shower.

"C'mon, Z, get your ass moving. I thought you were worried about sand in unmentionable places?"

"For fuck sakes, stop talking about my ass and my unmentionables." Zander grumbled as he stepped into the small bathroom. "You're really starting to creep me out."

It was crowded and he was very much aware of Zander's presence in the confined room but even more aware of the way Symone's ass rubbed against his cock as he set her on her feet. He couldn't even think of a half-decent comeback to Zander's complaint, as Symone turned and grabbed his hard cock, squeezing it lightly. It was the only thing his brain could wrap around at the moment.

"I want to see your unmentionable," Symone pleaded. To his disappointment, she released his dick and turned slightly toward Zander, her eyes sweeping down his body in a blatant invitation. "Yours too." She purred.

When her eyes returned to his, the naughty glint that had been in her eyes earlier had turned to pure devilish.

"What the hell are we waiting for then?" He grasped the hem of her cover-up, pulled it off then threw it behind him. "You can look, touch, do whatever the hell you want with my unmentionables."

Zander pushed past them and started the shower, causing Marco to chuckle again as he twisted his body in an odd angle to avoid making any contact with him.

The first night they had all been together he'd been so consumed by lust that he barely remembered whether he'd come in contact with Zander or not. Surely, they must have.

While he had been sketching earlier, he had seen the way Zander had looked at him. Deep in thought, Zander had nibbled his bottom lip with a confused look in his dark eyes. Had he been thinking of the offers Marco had only been half teasing about? If he had to guess, he'd say yes, and the thought of that only increased his desire to push the man to find out if he was in fact correct.

Soft hands brushed against his stomach as Symone began lowering his shorts. All thoughts of Zander fled. She looked up at him from under her thick lashes.

"Whatever I want, huh?"

He hissed as the material of his shorts scrapped against his engorged shaft. The hiss turned to a sigh as she pushed them past his hips and let them fall to the floor. He stepped out of them, kicking them to the side as he reached for the strings to her bikini top. Zander was already pushing down the bottoms of her bikini, at the same time steering her into the shower.

Zander began washing Symone's dark locks the instant they were under the spray. Marco, impatient to get his mouth on her, grabbed the soap and washed her chest and stomach. The water washed away the suds until only clear droplets sluiced down her body. As he quickly scrubbed away the sand from his own body, he leaned in and chased the water droplets rolling down her luscious body with his tongue. Down her collarbone to the swell of her breasts, he lapped at her skin until he reached one of her hardened nipples. He teased it with the tip of his tongue before sucking it into his mouth. Symone moaned as he sucked on the tender flesh and made him look up. They both stared at him as he sucked. The combination of their heated gazes made his hard shaft swell even further.

"God, that's hot," Zander groaned.

Fuck yeah it was hot, even more so with them watching. The exhibitionist in him was thrilled at having an audience, and without dropping his gaze, he moved across Symone's chest and lavished her other tight nub with teeth and tongue.

Symone began to tremble and moan as he moved farther down her body. He licked a path down her stomach, smiling against her skin when she gasped as he flicked his tongue into her navel. He made a mental note of that erogenous spot for later use. For now he had one target in mind and wouldn't be distracted.

Zander encouraged Symone to lean back, his large hands spreading her thighs further apart as Marco made his way down her body. His mouth watered at the thought of his prize spread out before him. He went to his knees, licked and sucked at her tender flesh as Zander began thrusting, pushing her harder against Marco's mouth. The sweet taste of her juices on his tongue drove him to seek out more of the addicting flavor.

Symone's whimpers turned to long drawn-out moans as he worked his fingers inside her slit, stroking the slick walls. God she was so tight. Her inner muscles clamped down on his fingers as if to pull them further inside. He wanted to bury himself inside her depths, wanted to be engulfed in her molten heat more than anything, but he pushed aside his own desires and concentrated on her pleasure. He sucked gently at her clit, teasing it with soft flicks of his tongue and kisses.

He couldn't help but feel a swell of pride bubble up in him that Symone was already reduced to incoherent babbling and a steady stream of pleas. The cocky side to his personality spurred him to double his efforts until she went out of her head.

As Symone's body began to tremble even harder, Zander changed the position of his hands. He gripped her thighs, lifting her up off the shower floor and spread her even wider. Marco sat back on his heels, continuing to pump his fingers in and out. Symone's legs draped over Zander's muscular forearms. The change in position exposed Zander's thick shaft as it pressed against Marco's fingers. The image before him nearly knocked him on his ass. It was so powerful. He looked up Symone's body. Her head was thrown back against Zander's shoulder and he was devouring her mouth in what looked like a consuming kiss.

Hell no! If she was going to be consumed it was going to be by his talents, not Zander's. One thing he'd always prided himself on was always being prepared and he was thankful he'd had the insight to drop a couple of condoms on the tile shelf. He slowed his thrusting digits with intent to keep her on the edge without pushing her over it. With his teeth, he tore open the condom package and rolled it on. He went to his feet. In one swift movement, he removed his fingers and thrust deep inside her. The combined effect of Symone breaking the kiss and crying out in pleasure and the feel of Zander's cock against his sac had Marco's eyes rolling back in his head.

"Son of a bitch," Zander huffed, as he was shoved against the tiled wall as Marco began to snap his hips.

"Oh, God… More." Symone's fingernails dug into the skin of his back, urging him to increase his thrusts.

Marco placed a hand on either side of Symone's and Zander's heads and locked eyes with Zander. "You heard her. I'm a fucking god," he taunted. He emphasized each word with a hard thrust.

He saw the defiant rage in Zander's dark eyes, mixing and battling with lust and need. Each movement of Marco's body forced Symone's ass back against Zander, at the perfect angle to ensure that each thrust forced Zander's hard shaft against Marco's balls. The defiance was quickly replaced until only the lust and hunger remained.

Marco stared into those black eyes—his own need pushed higher and higher. Zander's cock against his balls, the tight heat of Symone's channel scorching his cock, had him fighting to hold back the orgasm rushing down his spine. He was determined to feel not only her orgasm but Zander's before giving into his own.

He doubled his efforts, thrusting hard and fast into Symone, the rhythm increasing the friction on Zander's hard cock. He wasn't sure he could take much more before he lost it, his cock so fucking hard it was going to burst, his sac full and heavy from the dual stimulation.

"Oh fucking hell!" Zander grunted as the hot rush of his release bathed Marco's balls. The added heat ripped Marco's release out of him so suddenly, it consumed every fiber of his being. He could only give into the pleasure and ride it out with each pulse of his orgasm, made all the more intense when Symone's cry of pleasure filled the air.

Chapter Eleven

The sounds of an engine revving, followed by gravel under tires was the deciding factor in Zander's debate of getting up or rolling over and sleeping for a while longer.

The sounds emitting from the other side of the bed told him all he needed to know about who was lying next to him. Needless to say, the deep masculine snore wasn't the one he had been hoping for. In fact, it down right pissed him off that he'd found himself in the exact same position he'd been in the last time he'd spent the night with Marco and Symone. He didn't have a single complaint about the night before, hell at one point he'd thought his head would blow off with the intensity of their lovemaking, but for fuck's sake did it have to be the arrogant prick he always had to wake up next to? Was it too much to ask for an early morning cuddle? It wasn't like he was asking for another go round, though he wouldn't be opposed to that scenario either. The one playing out at the moment was not high on his wish list. Dammit, it didn't even make it on the fucking list.

Another thing gnawed at him like a dog on a bone — why the hell did Marco keep coming onto him? It was as if the son of a bitch knew the exact moment to touch or taunt, and leave him questioning just what the hell it was that was making him so goddamn excited.

What do you mean, what has you excited? It's Symone, you jackass. When have you ever been turned on by a dude?

About damn time, the rational side made its presence known in his fuddled brain. Of course it was Symone. Then again... *Oh hell no!* That wasn't even worth his consideration. The way he'd taken Symone to new heights of pleasure when he'd finally taken her to bed was all the evidence he needed as to what — more importantly — *who* had rocked his world. He pried his lids open and glanced toward the mound next to him.

It certainly wasn't you, Polo!

He was glad that was finally sorted out, now about Symone. This was the second time she'd snuck out after they'd been together. What was it she was running from? She was obviously trying to avoid an awkward morning after, but why? *How the hell could you get to know someone if you kept taking off before the talking?* Even he knew the impossibilities in that.

Symone was a complicated puzzle he intended to figure out. She tried to act blasé about everything, and he knew when someone was keeping all emotions out of the equation. He'd played that part often enough, hell he'd mastered it. Picking up women and seducing them into his bed had been his favorite pastime up until recently.

Symone, on the other hand, was a rookie. She couldn't hide the blush that showed like a flashing neon sign across her cheeks. She tried to act tough as nails, as if she were out for some sexual adventure, but underneath the carefree façade was one hell of a sweetheart. Soft, caring, and no matter how she tried to disguise it, part of her real personality shone through. That was the part he was most attracted to, the one he couldn't get enough of. That and the loneliness in her called out to him.

Well, well, well. Isn't today quite the day of introspection?

First, the self-assurance that he had zero attraction to men. And now the revelation that for the first time he was attracted to something more than nice tits and a sweet ass. He'd give his thoughts of Symone and his growing feelings for her a more in-depth analysis when he got some alone time. Right now, he could get rid of at least one of his concerns. Zander rolled to his side, reached out and shoved lightly at Marco. "Hey, Polo, time to get up." The sooner he got the man out of his house the better.

The sound coming from Marco was only slightly better than the snoring. He shoved at him a little harder. "Come on, get up."

"Why?" Marco asked sleepily. He didn't make any move to get up, In fact the son of a bitch snuggled further into the mattress and tightened the covers around him.

"It's time to take your ass home. I got shit to do today."

"I'm tired, why don't you come over here and snuggle my ass and go back to sleep?" Marco said in a way more sincere tone than Zander was comfortable with.

He was so not in the mood for anymore of Marco's bullshit. He only had to ease his leg up just a bit, flex his foot and… Shove. The loud thud as Marco hit the hardwood floor was very satisfying.

"What the hell?" Marco stuttered angrily as he pulled himself to a sitting position.

Zander flopped onto his back, a broad smile on his face. He stretched his arms high over his head and yawned. "Just showing you what I wanted to do to your ass."

"That's not what you were thinking last night." Marco snarled.

He ignored the innuendo and relegated it to the basket he titled, *'Another dose of Marco bullshit'*. "Yeah, well, that's what I wanted to do with your ass at this moment," he replied nonchalantly.

Marco hauled himself to his feet and inhaled sharply. Zander tensed, waiting for him to pounce. The easy smile stayed on his face, but he was more than ready if it was going to get physical. His eyes shifted back to Marco. He was bristling with anger. His face was a deep shade of red as he glared at him. Zander could read the concentration as if Marco was calculating the risks and benefits. His smile grew even wider. *Bring it.*

Marco's eyes scanned the room before settling back on his. "Where the hell is Symone?"

"They say the short-term memory is the first to go," he teased.

"What the hell is that supposed to mean?"

Zander heard the annoyance and ignored it. "I told you last time. The sounds coming out from you at night are enough to make anyone run and hide." He arched an eyebrow at him. "You ever thought about seeing a professional about your problem?"

Marco's growl came from deep in his throat. His stance was one of aggression, feet wide apart, hands on his hips, but Zander couldn't quite take it seriously. It was just too hard to take a man soberly when he was buck-ass naked and sporting morning wood. Zander started to chuckle.

"Fuck you," Marco bit out then turned and stormed out of the room.

Marco's comeback didn't need a response but he laughed uproariously. He couldn't help it. Marco's cocky attitude amused the hell out of him sometimes, and when he got the upper hand on him? Every time.

The sound of the bathroom door slamming hard enough to shake the walls struck him as even funnier than Marco trying to be badass. He laughed until his stomach muscles ached and still he couldn't stop the laughter that held him in its grasp.

Once he'd gotten himself under control, he rolled out of bed and raked a hand through his hair. His bedroom looked as if a tornado had gone through it. Clothes were strewn everywhere, the nightstand drawer hung precariously from its track and the smell of sex was still thick in the air.

He heard the shower turn on and his body reacted immediately. Heat surged through him and his semi-hard shaft swelled as he recalled how intense the shower he'd shared with Marco and Symone had been. No fucking way was he going to admit it to himself, let alone Marco, that it had been the hottest thing he'd ever experienced.

The way Marco had looked at him as he'd thrust into Symone, forcing her back against his cock, had been staggering. Just another thing he was going to have to give some thought to when he got a moment alone. He needed some time to work out whatever the hell was going on between the three of them, and just exactly what he intended to do about the situation.

Putting the confusing thoughts on the back burner for the moment, he snatched a pair of shorts out of the small dresser and slipped them on. Coffee, he needed coffee. He headed to the kitchen, his only purpose to get enough caffeine in him before he had to deal with Marco again.

Thanks to the two-minute brew time on his Bunn, Zander was working on his second cup of coffee when Marco strolled into the kitchen, towel around his waist, body still dripping wet. He didn't say a word as he walked to the coffee pot and poured coffee into a cup Zander had set out for him, all the while running a towel over his damp hair.

Marco brought his coffee to the table and flopped down in the chair across from him. "So what's the plan?"

"Other than getting you the hell out of here, don't have any." He sipped his coffee.

"Don't be a bitch," Marco grunted as he sipped his own coffee. "Hey, this is good." He took another sip before continuing, "I was talking about what we're going to do about Symone and her inability to sleep in?"

"Oh come on. You know exactly what she is doing, and it has nothing to do with sleep. You've played the game."

Marco's eyes narrowed. "The game?"

"You know, the one where you sneak out to avoid the awkward morning after."

"I wouldn't know about that," Marco responded lightly, still sipping his coffee.

While Zander knew Marco was insufferable, he couldn't believe the man had the gall to try to bullshit another player. "Are you always this full of shit or do you work at it extra hard for my benefit?" he asked curiously.

Marco chuckled and set his mug down on the table. "Nah, what you see is what you get. But, seriously I kind of like the morning after." He waggled his brows at Zander. "A little morning loving always puts me in a good mood and some company for coffee and breakfast never was a bad thing either."

He stared at him, disbelieving. "Isn't that just giving them false hope? I mean I've seen you around and not once have I seen a girl on your arm a second time."

Marco waved him off with a hand. "The moment you buy them a drink, many of them are already hoping. I'm honest up front so what does it matter when you bail?"

Zander was ready with a nasty response but snapped his mouth shut. Marco had a point. As much as he hated to admit it, he wasn't that much different from him — only the time that they walked away from the conquest was different.

He'd never really thought much about their feelings. He always believed that as long as he was honest up front and everyone had a good time, he wasn't doing anything wrong. For the first time in his life, the shoe was on the other foot, and he didn't like the fit at all.

Zander stood abruptly and went to pour another cup of coffee. Women had always been a form of entertainment, sexual tools used to satisfy his occasional need for something more substantial than his own hand. It had meant nothing to him. Never once had he thought about how they might feel. It made him sick to think about how he had treated women in the past and his desire to escape being the focus of the topic was paramount. "So why haven't you bailed on Symone yet?"

"Simple. I plan on marrying her," Marco responded in a matter-of-fact tone.

Zander spun around, choking on his coffee. The hot liquid landing on his bare chest caused him to grunt in pain. "What did you say?" he asked in disbelief as he grabbed a towel and wiped down his chest. He couldn't have heard him right.

"Something wrong with your hearing, Z? I said I plan on marrying her." He waved a hand between them. "This thing we got going on right now is fun. One hot sexual adventure I'm personally enjoying the hell out of and I don't mind sharing her for the time being. But eventually she's going to have to make a choice. I'm counting on it being me." The arrogant ass relaxed back in his chair and sipped his coffee as if he'd been talking about the weather or some other mundane topic.

"The hell you are!" Zander dumped his coffee, mug and all in the sink and moved back to the table. He placed his hand on the hard surface and leaned in toward Marco. "What the hell makes you think she would want an arrogant prick like you? And secondly"—he narrowed his eyes. Jealousy caused his blood to boil, anger prickled at his skin—"over my dead body."

Marco gripped the arms of his chair and leaned in, glaring at Zander, a dangerous glint in his eyes.

Not fucking scared, buddy. He'd be damned if he'd let Marco get the upper hand in this. Sure as shit wasn't even going to entertain the possibility of him besting him? The moment lingered, neither willing to back down or show an ounce of fear.

"Fuck, you're sexy when you get riled up." Marco moved the last couple of inches and pecked him on the lips before taking up his relaxed position again.

Zander's eyes went wide. He was too stunned to even retaliate. "Hey, what the fuck," he sputtered as he swiped a hand across his mouth in disgust.

"What? You are sexy when you're mad," he said easily. "And don't tell me you're surprised to hear I want Symone for more than a romp in the hay. Haven't you been thinking the same thing?"

Zander fell into his chair, still reeling from both the kiss and Marco's declaration.

Marco was damn lucky he hadn't found himself picking up his sorry ass off the floor. Had he not just dropped the marriage bomb on him, knocking him off-kilter, he was sure he would have given in to his initial reaction to the kiss and punched him in his too-smug face. A little peck seemed insignificant when compared to the concept of Marco marrying Symone. He barely knew her, for Christ sakes. How the hell did someone come to the conclusion that another person was marriage material after a couple of dates? Unless...

He clenched his hands into tights fists as another wave of jealousy raced through him. Had Symone and Marco been seeing each other more than he knew about? He gave himself an internal shake and dismissed that crazy notion before it went any further.

Symone had been reluctant to come to his house, had fervently insisted that Marco be there or she wouldn't show. She might be trying to keep herself detached but she was struggling with it.

She needs us together.

It made perfect sense. The first week the calls had been fun, an easy getting to know each other type of chatter. After they had all spent the night together she had avoided all personal subjects, add in the fact that she refused to see either of them separately and *bingo*!

Well, I'll be damned.

Zander rose, casually making his way to the sink and retrieved his mug. He poured another cup and took a sip. He turned and leaned against the counter, and without saying a word simply stared at his opponent.

Let the battle begin.

After the silence stretched to an uncomfortable level, Marco straightened and growled. "Well?"

"Frankly, it's difficult to take you seriously."

"Take me seriously?" Marco replied happily. "Oh, you can bet your sweet candy ass I'm serious."

He shot Marco a disbelieving look over the rim of his mug. "About the kiss or the marriage?"

"The marriage maybe." He laughed before he leaned back in his chair and downed the rest of his coffee. "But I definitely want another kiss and I always get what I want." He turned and left the kitchen.

Zander was still chuckling when Marco returned from the bedroom dressed. He was able to get himself under control long enough to follow him out onto the porch. He watched Marco make his way to his car before he yelled, "One more thing."

Marco turned around, the arrogant smile firmly in place. "Yes, sweetheart?"

"If you ever try to kiss me again, I'll kick your ass."

It was Marco's turn to laugh boisterously. "I didn't try, honey. I did." He got into his car, then slammed the door and drove away, still laughing.

Zander stood there, mouth agape.

Why, that no-good, arrogant, cocky, insufferable, crazy fucking...

"I hate that man!" He walked back into the house, contemplating the dependability of a mercy killing defense.

Chapter Twelve

Symone stood in her kitchen trying to hold back the tears and dislodge the lump in her throat as she brushed her fingers reverently over the dark mahogany frame.

Marco's painting of her was astonishing, heart-stopping, magnificent... Hell she couldn't come up with a word that would do justice to something as exquisite as the masterpiece before her. She'd always been a fan of Edward Hopper, William James and more recently David Ligare, whose paintings captured humanist beauty so realistically they left her questioning if they were paintings, not photographs.

Still, Marco's art surpassed them all in her eyes. The ache in her chest became increasingly painful as she stared at her painting.

For the past week, she'd been able to avoid both men. She'd ignored their calls, letting them go straight to voicemail without listening to them. Each bouquet of flowers, she'd accepted and thanked the delivery boy for, but had never once thanked the senders. This newest gift, however, forced her to turn away in overwhelming guilt.

"How the hell do players do this shit?" she asked aloud in her empty apartment.

It was easy to admit to herself that she was beginning to care about both of them. They were unique. Each brought something to her life that she had always looked for.

Marco the protector, with a tender soft side, and Zander with his wit and intellect that always kept her thinking.

Individually, they were each great men. Together they took her to heights of pleasure she hadn't known existed. Yet, no matter how nice they were, how sexy or downright fucking gorgeous, she wasn't willing to give into these feelings of caring for and missing them. Maybe what she needed was another night out at Menjo's, to find some arrogant bastard who could help her forget about them.

Her internal rant was interrupted by a knock on her front door. *Great! It better not be either one of them or so help me God…*

"C'mon, Symone, open up. I gotta pee," Sedesa yelled through the door.

Relieved that it was her best friend, Symone unlocked and opened the front door. "Hey, Sedes."

Sedesa pushed past her and stopped dead in her tracks. "Holy shit! What did you do, rob a florist? There has to be like ten bouquets here. The only other place I've seen this many flowers was at a…"

"Fifteen actually, or at least I think so. I quit counting."

Sedesa spun, a horrified look on her face. "Oh my God, please tell me it wasn't Grandpa Adams."

"No one died, Sedes," she assured her friend. "I think the guys are now competing for the title of who can buy out the florist first." She waved a hand at the vases of roses, carnations, wildflowers and the numerous other varieties she had no idea of what their names were. "Either that or the title of who can waste the most money."

"Wow. All these from just Marco and Zander?" Sedesa leaned down and sniffed the newest edition to the group. A vase of lavender roses. The delivery boy had informed Symone that the lavender rose was chosen by those wishing to make an impact with a unique and extraordinary flower. They'd made an impact all right. Somehow, she doubted that the impact Marco had been trying to make was taking up the last available surface in her home.

"That's nothing, check out the painting in the dining room."

"Painting? Is it the one you were telling me Marco did of you?" Sedesa inquired as she walked to the dining room.

"Yeah that's…"

"Oh my God!"

"…it," she finished her sentence as she moved up next to Sedesa, who was jumping up and down as if she'd swallowed a truck load of Mexican jumping beans.

"It's amazing. Do you think he'd paint me?" She stopped jumping long enough to reach out as if to touch the painting.

Symone slapped her hand down before she could actually touch it. "Don't touch it. It's going back." She turned and headed into the living room and flopped down on the couch.

"Are you out of your ever frickin' mind?" Sedesa shouted as she hurried along behind her and sat next to her on the couch. "You can't send it back."

"Yes I can. I can't keep something like that when I have no plans to ever see him again," she replied calmly.

Sedesa's eyes went wide. "Again I ask, are you out of your ever frickin' mind? Why wouldn't you want to see him again? The man is smoking hot and talented to boot." She pushed out her lips in an exaggerated pout. "Besides, I want a painting for Ian. Can't you at least date him long enough for that?"

Symone swatted playfully at her deranged friend. "Your pout has no effect on me. It hasn't since we were sixteen and you used it to talk me into sneaking out."

"Oh the look on your face when the siren and flashy lights went off was priceless." Sedesa chuckled.

So was the look on her mom's face when the cops had brought her to their front door. She'd been grounded for years for that stunt. At sixteen, two weeks had felt like years anyway. The full context of Sedesa's statement hit her. "You're still seeing Ian?"

"Well, yeah." Sedesa leaned back on the couch and propped her feet up on the flower-covered coffee table. "I'm cooking him dinner tonight."

Symone's jaw nearly hit her thighs. "What? When the hell did you learn to cook?"

Sedesa cooking? This, she had to see. No way would she actually taste it but she'd pay good money to see Sedesa standing over a stove.

"Ian's been teaching me," she said with a smirk. "Last night he tried to teach me to cook a roast."

She arched an eyebrow at her. "Tried?"

Sedesa glanced up at her, a little pink starting to color her cheeks. "The roast won, but I have high hopes for the baked flounder. Ian says it's foolproof."

Symone snorted and shook her head. "Whatever. Let me know how that works out for you," she muttered as she reached down and grabbed her purse from the floor. After a moment of scrounging around, she finally pulled out her small calendar and pen. She laughed as she circled today's date.

"What the hell are you doing?" Sedesa asked curiously.

"Recording the day hell froze over."

"Bite me, bitch," Sedesa replied, no real anger in her voice. She stuck her tongue out.

Symone chuckled and smiled. She returned her calendar to her purse, and when she looked back at Sedesa, her expression was serious.

"I think he may be the one," she whispered.

"You barely know him, Sedes. Hell, he's already trying to change you. He's making you learn to cook for Christ sakes."

"I didn't say he *was* the one, just that he may be the one. I know when I'm with him he makes me feel things I've never felt before. And you're right, he is making me learn to cook, but not for the reason you think. Ian loves to cook and I want to share that with him. He may give the appearance that he's cocky and carefree but underneath the tough-guy exterior is a real sweetheart." She reached over and tugged at Symone's hair. "Kind of like someone else I know."

Symone had never heard Sedesa talk seriously about anyone since high school. It was one of the things she'd always been envious about. Sedesa could go out and have a good time and never really experienced heartbreak.

Her stomach rolled at the thought of her friend having to experience such pain for the first time. Symone remembered how it had felt like her heart was being ripped out of her chest when her high-school sweetheart, Kyle, had dumped her on prom night. He had left her on the dance floor in search of someone who would be, in his words, more understanding of his physical needs. She'd been a virgin and had planned on saving herself for marriage. What a naïve twit she'd been. The heartache from Kyle had been nothing compared to the agony and shame when she'd given her virginity to Greg in college. Like Sedesa now, she had thought he might be *the one*.

After weeks of dating, she'd finally given herself to him. He'd been nothing like the caring man she had thought he was. Once they were in bed together, Greg had turned hard and aggressive. He had taken his pleasure without any thought for her inexperience or pain. Afterward, he'd left her crying, tossing over his shoulder, "Thanks for a good time," before walking out of the door.

As bad as that whole experience had been, she didn't even want to think about how Travis had treated her. Hoped to God, Sedesa never found out what it felt like to have someone betray her love. She'd do anything to protect her friend from any kind of misery or pain.

"Love really isn't all it's cracked up to be. Can't you just enjoy Ian like you have the others in the past?"

"Oh, Boo," Sedesa replied softly, using the nickname she'd given Symone when they were kids, and laid her head on her shoulder. "I know it can suck. I've been there every time someone hurt you, but remember how much fun you had with Kyle in your junior, and into the senior year? Hell, look how amazing your relationship with Travis was in the beginning. Would you really want to give up all the great times we had, the trips, the year of good times?"

Symone felt tears sting at the back of her eyes as she tried to figure out if the good really was worth the bad. "I don't know," she finally admitted.

"At this moment, I think a year of laughing and loving with Ian would be worth it. Who knows, maybe I'll get lucky and get it right the first time. Maybe he won't break my heart. It reminds me of that song we used to like."

"Which one?"

"The one by Garth Brooks that said something about life being better left to chance. Missing the pain, but then missing the dance, or however it went." Sedesa looked up, released her hand and wiped away a tear that had escaped even with Symone's best effort to hold it back. "I want to go to the dance, Boo."

"And here I thought you were the smarter one of us." She kissed Sedesa's nose. "You're still the sappy one."

Sedesa laughed and kissed her cheek. "Whatever. I've never met a bigger sap than you. If you were the smart one, you wouldn't be sitting here on this couch with me. You'd be thanking that gorgeous, talented hunk of yours in person."

"I thought you had to pee?" she questioned, not wanting to discuss Marco or Zander.

"Nah, I just said that so you would hurry up. Good attempt to change the subject, by the way. When are you going to see Marco and thank him? Oh and don't forget to thank Zander too. He did after all send you half these flowers." A mischievous glint entered her

Essence of the Challenge

eyes. "Want me to go with you? I can record the thank you for prosperity?"

"You're such a pervert."

"I prefer the term deviant diva. It sounds…I don't know, less pervy."

Snorting, Symone pushed Sedesa off her and stood. "Go home, Miss Deviant Diva. I have an appointment in an hour I have to get ready for."

"Then are you going to thank those two gods?"

She placed her hands on her hips and gave Sedesa a mock scowl. "If I say yes will you leave?"

Sedesa jumped to her feet. "I'm already gone." She giggled as she headed toward the door. "Have fun and don't do anything I wouldn't do."

"That's a pretty short list," she muttered under her breath.

"I heard that," Sedesa called out. "Call me later. We can compare notes, my baked flounder versus your hot tamales."

Symone heard her laughter as she shut the door. Shaking her head at Sedesa's piss-poor attempt at humor, she headed to her bedroom to get ready for her four o'clock appointment.

Normally she would have been grumbling about such a late appointment to check out a new property. Sometimes the homeowners wanted to show her every nook and cranny instead of the highlights and she could be there for hours.

Tonight she was looking forward to a drawn-out meeting. The longer it took, the more time she had to think about what she wanted to do about Marco and Zander.

* * * *

As he stood on the small deck overlooking the community pool, Zander was oblivious to the activity below him. Over the last week, he'd been unable to concentrate on anything other than Symone and what exactly he wanted from her.

Carefree, no-commitment types of relationship had always been enough for him. A relationship wasn't actually a term he should be using since one-night stands hardly constituted a relationship.

He'd made it through high school, college and beyond without any messy emotional ties. He wasn't against them, hell his parents had married when his mom had been seventeen and his dad had been twenty. They were still together, and from what he could tell were very happy. He'd just never really had the desire to have anyone in his life as more than acquaintances. Until now. Symone made him think about things. Things like having more, being more, and crazy shit like love.

If he were completely honest with himself, Symone wasn't the only one occupying his thoughts as of late. Marco was also on his mind a great deal.

It was hard not to think of Symone without also thinking about the irritating man who he deemed as his rival. And, since he *was* being completely honest with himself, he'd have to admit that he was beginning to see Marco as more than just *the competition*.

As much as he hated it, he respected the hell out of the man. Under different circumstances, he could even see the two of them becoming good friends. They had easily agreed that Symone was trying her damnedest to see them as nothing more than a sexual adventure. More importantly, they agreed that it really wasn't her style and was having a difficult time keeping her emotions out of it. They could easily use that to their advantage. Again there was the term, *theirs*. Not Zander's advantage or Marco's — *theirs* — as if they were a team.

As long as Symone didn't see them as individuals, it would be easier for her to keep the fantasy going and it explained why she now even refused to talk to them separately on the phone. And just like that, they were working together to force her to see them as something beyond a good time.

A truce, for the time being, was agreed upon. The next weapon in their arsenal was to combine forces to achieve their goal. Zander wasn't particularly happy about it, but what other options were there at this point? Their solo efforts had not been successful. Marco seemed thrilled as hell about the two of them becoming allies. They agreed to work together for the greater good.

The plan to lure Symone, under false pretenses, to look at a property for potential sale had been Zander's idea. It was foolproof. Only one problem existed with his plan.

Since Symone had already been to his home, she would know it was a setup the moment she turned off Highway Nineteen into his private drive, so he needed Marco in order for his plan to succeed. Both had acknowledged and consented to the armistice, but it didn't mean he liked it. Or could admit that he liked it.

"I still don't understand why you get to answer the door, it's my fucking house," Marco grumbled as he walked out onto the deck and handed Zander a beer.

He took it and drew a long draw from the bottle. "Let me explain it again in terms your pea brain can understand. We flipped a coin, I called heads —"

"About that," Marco interrupted angrily. "No way can you be that goddamn lucky all the time, Z-Man. Let me see that coin."

He shrugged and reached in his right front pocket. He pulled out a quarter and flipped it to Marco. "I think my feelings are hurt, heartbroken even, that you would think I would cheat you." Utter disbelief colored his words. He blinked at Marco innocently.

"In a heartbeat and for a hell of a lot less than the chance to get your hands on Symone first," Marco accused. He studied the quarter in his hand, flipping it back and forth. "Still think you're fucking with me," he complained as he stuffed the quarter in his pocket.

He shot Marco a look. "Keep it," he said flatly. "I'm just a lucky guy, what can I say?"

"You better hope that luck of yours holds up," Marco said easily as he took another pull from his beer. "She's going to be pissed you lied to her."

He snickered, knowing he'd already thought of that scenario. "It's your house. I'm just an innocent bystander."

"Bastard." Marco clinked his beer against his. "Here's to your luck."

The sound of the doorbell cut off any reply he would have made. He set his bottle down on a small table and looked at Marco. "You just remember the other part of our cease-fire agreement. If this works out as we planned, you keep your damn hands to yourself."

"Oh, babe, my hands, lips, tongue and Mr. Happy plan on being very busy. And not on myself." Marco laughed heartily.

Zander narrowed his eyes at him. "You know what I mean, keep them the fuck off *me*."

Marco huffed slightly and gave him a mischievous smile. "Aww, you're no fun. How am I supposed to resist such a hot, sexy stud like you?"

"Wait a minute! Mr. Happy?" he asked, wrinkling his nose in disgust. He shook his head, leaving Marco laughing and following behind him as he went to answer the door.

With his right hand, he rubbed the coin in his left front pocket. *C'mon, Lady Luck, don't fail me now.*

Chapter Thirteen

On the short drive to the Sandpiper Gulf Front Condominiums, the talk with Sedesa as well as the song *The Dance* kept playing over and over in Symone's head.

It was easy for her friend to see the benefits in a relationship. While Sedesa had never had to deal with the truly ugly side of relationships, she did make some valid points.

The first nine months with Travis had been probably some of the most fun-filled times she'd had since moving to Florida. Every day had been an adventure. Discovering each other's mind as well as body had been exciting. The weekend they had spent together at Disney World had been two solid days of laughter. She and Travis had both returned from that trip with aching muscles, from laughing and loving to the fullest. There had been other getaway weekends that were just as memorable, and plenty of quiet evenings at home that she cherished.

Was the pain really worth those good times?

Thinking about it now, with the pain diminished, less raw, she could easily answer yes. Six months ago, the answer would have been different.

Even if she did allow herself to feel something for Marco and Zander, how in the hell could she choose between them?

Who are you kidding? You are already feeling something for them and you're too afraid.

And, so what if she was? There was no way she could choose between them so it was a moot point anyway. A camaraderie was beginning to blossom between Zander and Marco, but it was tentative at best. She was the prize in their competition and she just couldn't see the two of them shaking hands and suddenly agreeing to be one big, happy love triangle.

How did something like that work beyond the bedroom anyway? A relationship between two people was hard enough to manage. Three distinct personalities merging into a taboo lifestyle had to be downright impossible.

Symone pulled into an empty parking spot in front of the condo complex and cut the engine. Leaning her head back against the headrest, she struggled to pull her thoughts off the two distractions in her life and try to focus on her job.

Closing her eyes, she took a deep breath then let it out slowly. Images of Marco entering her over and over as he fucked her against Zander and the shower wall filled her mind. Her eyes snapped open and she sat upright.

Bad idea. Okay, no closing your eyes.

The way they had worked together in pleasuring her, hell the three of them together, was amazing.

Wait... Why can't I have both?

They didn't need to set up a formal arrangement or anything, but at least let things happen naturally and see where they could go, for as long as possible. It wasn't like they were talking marriage or long-term commitment, but she wasn't going to rule it out either.

Just three people getting to know each other, sharing some laughs. She shouldn't be thinking about hearts, flowers and broken hearts before even giving it a chance.

And don't forget the toe-curling, all-encompassing, and oh-my-fucking-God sex.

She laughed, as if she could ever forget that part of it.

She suddenly felt better than she had in a long, long while. In a blink of an eye, it all became so clear. Instead of trying to be something she wasn't, aka a player, for the first time she was going into a *relationship* without thinking long-term.

No expectations seemed more reasonable and attainable than unemotional. After meeting the clients, she'd call Marco, thank him for the painting and invite him and Zander out for dinner. Perhaps drinks...or they could jump right to dessert. No expectations did not mean she couldn't hope for something right?

Excited with the conclusion she'd come to and no longer wanting to draw out the appointment, she grabbed the stats on the Sandpiper Gulf Front Condominiums.

A large outdoor swimming pool with full sun exposure during the day, surrounded by a huge deck, perfect for relaxing, socializing or just reading that perfect novel.

Who comes up with this shit?

Of course it's exposed to sun. Wouldn't that be the point?

A 'sunny location'.
Tennis court.
Shuffleboard.
Storage on ground level for owners.

Okay this was just stupid. *Sunny location? Of course it's sunny. It's Florida for God's sake and storage for owners? Who else would they supply them for?* She shook her head, moving on to the basics.

All the condos at Sandpiper were two-bedroom, two-bath and both inside and corner units were thirteen hundred-seventy-five square feet. She'd be looking at a corner unit and the average selling price of other comparable units ran five-hundred thousand and ninety-nine dollars.

Good luck getting that in this recession.

Symone stuffed the paperwork into her briefcase and straightened her suit. Leaving home, she had hoped this meeting would drag on, now she didn't care about square footage, sunny pools or anything else. She only wanted to get home and call Marco and Zander.

Guess that old saying is true – be careful what you wish for.

She stepped out of the car with her business face on, eager to get this over as quickly as possible. She critically scanned the property. The grounds leading up to the entrance lived up to their description in the pamphlet. The lawns were lush and beautifully manicured. The brick walkway was surrounded by flowing tropical bushes and towering majestic palms. A balmy sea breeze enveloped her with the scents of the ocean. Whoever had written the description had been sorely in need of a good editor, but the property itself was picturesque.

Symone's heated skin erupted in goosebumps the instant she stepped through the entrance doorway and was hit with a blast of cool air.

"Can I help you?" an elderly gentleman asked from behind a desk. He had a bright, welcoming smile on his wrinkled face.

She couldn't help but smile in return. "I hope you can. I'm Symone Adams. I have an appointment with…"

"Mr. Cantrell," he interrupted.

Stunned for a moment, Symone stared at him in confusion. Was she here to see Mr. Cantrell? Crap, she hadn't even looked at the name on the stat sheet. "Umm, yeah I think so." Obviously, she hadn't done so well putting on her agent persona. How the hell could she not know who she was meeting?

"I've been expecting you. You are here to view a unit for possible sale, aren't you?" he inquired.

"That obvious, huh?"

His smile grew. "It wasn't too hard even for an old geezer like me. You're not dressed for the beach. Mr. Cantrell informed me an agent would be arriving." He nodded toward her briefcase. "It's four o'clock. I didn't even need to pull out my *Hardy Boys Detective Handbook*."

"Got it in one." She winked. "Hardy who? Were those Nancy Drew's sidekicks?" she teased.

He looked aghast at her question. "The Hardy Boys Mystery Stories started in 1927. Nancy didn't come along until 1930."

"Yeah, but she made them look good," she taunted with a sly smile.

He shook his head at her obvious tease. "Mr. Cantrell is expecting you. Go on up, unit four-fourteen." He jabbed a thumb toward the elevators.

"Thank you." She moved in that direction.

"Miss Adams?"

Symone stopped and looked back over her shoulder. "Yes?"

"Women usually do make us look good."

She smiled then turned and pushed the button for the elevator. If she was very lucky, she would be making two of them look and feel real good sandwiched between them later.

The elevator doors opened, and she entered, pushing the button for the fourth floor. "That works both ways," she replied. She heard his deep laughter as the elevator doors closed.

Symone stepped off the elevator and walked down to the end of the hall. At unit four-fourteen she knocked on the door. After a brief silence, she could hear muffled laughter through the door. At least the owner sounded happy. Hopefully he'd still be that way when she told him what she thought his chances of selling in this market were.

She ran a hand down her skirt and adjusted the hem of her jacket as she waited. The door opened, and Symone's heart skipped a beat and her breath died in her throat. On the other side of the door, stood a very sexy, very smug-looking Zander.

She barely had time for the full effect of her shock to process when his strong arms wrapped around her and he pressed his lips against hers, demanding entrance.

As Symone opened to him, all thought fled as his tongue invaded her mouth and his strong hand caressed down her back. He grabbed her ass and pulled her hard against his body, massaging her flesh. With his other hand, he threaded his fingers through her hair and pulled her head back as he devoured her mouth. The sound he made sent her pulse racing.

A deep animalistic sound, even more than a growl, vibrated through her. Symone's mind may not have caught up but her body knew exactly what it wanted. She dropped her briefcase to clutch his shoulders and rub and slide against him as the kiss went on and on.

As soon as Zander broke the kiss, they were both panting and breathing each other in. She barely had a chance to catch a breath before Marco was pushing between them and pulling her against him.

"My turn," he growled, before taking her mouth.

His flavor mingled with Zander's as his tongue pushed past her lips. The effect left her reeling and wanting more. Marco's kiss was fierce and possessive. She didn't try to fight it. She finally submitted to the pleasure she had denied herself for the last week.

How could I have thought to give this up?

Only when her lungs screamed for oxygen did she pull away from the kiss, leaning hard against Marco as she fought to catch her breath. "I. Wait…" she forced out between pants.

"No more waiting," Zander replied as he pressed against her back and kissed her neck.

"He's right. We've waited long enough," Marco agreed.

They worked together moving her farther into the condo. For a brief moment, she thought of complaining. After all, they had lured her here. Set her up. She should be a little upset about that, shouldn't she?

As they continued to lead her, they both kissed and licked at her neck. She just couldn't find it in herself to question their motives, at least not at the moment.

I couldn't care less how the hell they set it up.

This was all about her new resolve to let the cards fall where they may. As they continued their assault on her neck, talk seemed overrated. They would have time to talk afterward. She had no plans to sneak away this time. In fact, unlike the previous times, she was determined to be a full participant, to not just sit back and let them pleasure her.

I want the full treatment of give and take this time.

Symone easily followed as they moved. She fisted the material of Marco's shirt in both hands. "What if I hadn't shown?"

"Plan B," Marco murmured against her flesh.

"Which is?"

"Kidnapping," Zander replied.

She burst out laughing. "You can't be serious."

They came to a halt and Marco straightened. His hazel eyes were dilated and dark, full of heat and hunger. "Completely, though if you want us to stop just say the word."

"We'll just move on to Plan C," Zander countered, still licking and nibbling at her neck.

Before she could ask, Marco placed a finger against her lips. "Don't ask and don't say no. Please." The last word was a deep husky whisper.

Zander's hand moved low on her belly. Excitement jolted and surged through her system. With the arousal flooding her body, the very thought of saying no was ludicrous. She placed a soft kiss against the skin of his finger before pushing it away. She sent him a sultry smile as she reached out, seeking the buttons of his shirt. "I had no intentions of saying no," she teased, popping the first button.

His eyes went wide, nostrils flaring on a sharp intake of breath. Encouraged, she worked her way down, unbuttoning each one, pulling his shirt free from the waistband of his jeans.

Marco covered her mouth with his, licking at her lips. He plunged deep into the kiss as her lips parted, his flavor and touch igniting her. Zander kissed up her neck, placing open-mouthed kisses across her cheek. His scent and demanding touch inflamed her.

The three of them became a frenzy of pulling, pushing and frantic hands awkwardly removing clothes without breaking the kiss or losing contact. A sigh escaped her lips as the last of the clothing fell to the floor. Her lips felt swollen, ached from Marco's claiming kiss. Marco began kissing down her neck, but she stopped him with a shaky hand as he reached her collarbone.

He glanced up at her with questioning, hazel eyes that melted her. She threaded her fingers through his silky blond strands. Her breath caught. The look on his face and hunger in his eyes was an invitation to sin.

"Symone." His voice was a mixture of barely controlled desire and uncertainty.

"My turn," she whispered, holding gaze. "I don't want to just feel pleasure." With her free hand, she reached back and fisted it in Zander's thick dark hair, pulling him closer. "I want to give it."

Chapter Fourteen

Delicious sparks of pain danced across his skull as Symone tugged his hair at the same time as a tickling sensation started at the base, inching its way down his spine. God, he couldn't get enough of her.

From the moment he'd first laid eyes on her he'd known there was something about her. Zander couldn't explain it, had no words for what he was feeling, but it went beyond physical.

There wasn't any logical explanation for it either. He just knew that when she was gone, his chest ached for her. When she was near him, he felt driven nearly out of his fucking mind with the need to bury himself deep inside her heat.

'I want to give it.'

Symone's declaration had sent a lightning strike straight to his cock. He molded his body to hers, hissing when his aching shaft connected with the smooth skin of her taut ass. She started kissing her way down

Marco's chest. Each excruciatingly slow inch forced her ass harder against his cock.

Oh fuck. She was burning him alive.

His balls drew up tight as he tried to back off from the overwhelming pleasure. Concentrating to slow his breathing down, he felt powerless and tried to think about programming.

Static memory...allocation...dynamic...arbitrary size... binary at compile-time...

It's not working!

Goddammit, not even boring programming shit could diminish the effects of the slide of Symone's body. She tugged his hair, forcing him to bend with her as the pressure increased. He clenched his jaw, tried to take deep breaths through his nose as he teetered on the edge.

"God, Symone, please," Marco groaned. "Suck me."

"Fuck." Zander ripped Symone's hand from his hair, forcing an inch between them. No fucking way was he shooting yet.

Breathe. He placed his hands on Symone's shoulders, encouraged her to her knees as he dropped to his. *Condom.*

He frantically searched for his pants. The sound of Symone's wet sucking noises and Marco's moans filled the air.

Fuck, I need a damn condom. He scrambled for his jeans, pulling one from the pocket.

"Yeah, baby, that's it. Use your tongue. Take me deep," Marco encouraged.

Bastard, shut the fuck up, please for God's sake.

Marco's deep husky voice and the memory of just how her full lips felt on his cock, how that talented tongue worked a hard shaft...

God, he was going to explode. He tore open the package, rolled the condom on while moving up behind her. He pushed his way between her parted knees. The soft, smooth skin of her thighs was like silk against his own.

Zander steadied her with a hand against her back, pushed her forward until she was right where he wanted her. He groaned as the head of his cock brushed against her crease, prodding until he encountered her wet slit.

Marco fisted Symone's long, dark hair and stopped the bobbing motion of her head. She whimpered in protest around his flesh. She pushed back, wiggled her hips enticingly. Zander looked up—black, feral eyes met his. Marco's lip curled into a sneer. "Take her, Z."

Whether it was an encouragement or a challenge, he didn't care. He thrust deep, in one hard snap of his hips, going balls-deep in tight, perfect heat. "Fuck, she's tight."

If he could suspend time, control his voracious hunger, he'd revel in the feel of their bodies united. How right it felt.

Symone's muffled cry of pleasure and the way she pushed her ass back against him, encouraged him to move, couldn't be ignored. Marco's fists tightened in her hair as a string of pleas, praises and curses tumbled from him while he fucked Symone's mouth.

Zander's control shattered. He grabbed her hips and pistoned in and out. Her tight channel gripped him. He felt her. Felt all of her, squeezing and burning him.

"So tight. Ah, God, so fucking perfect," Zander moaned.

This was going to be hard and fast. No fucking way could he endure the sweet torture. Each day since he'd last seen her his need had grown. His own hand did nothing to slake his desire, but only intensified what he wanted most.

Later, he'd bring her pleasure over and over—right now, at this moment, it was primal. His focus narrowed down until the only thing he knew was pleasure. The only thing he felt was the perfect slide of slick heat against every inch of his shaft, stroking him.

"Close... Now... Right fucking now!" Marco roared.

Zander's eyes rolled back in his head as white heat raced down his spine. One last thrust, and he let go. His tight grip on Symone's hips was the only thing keeping him anchored as he rode each wave of his orgasm. He was only distantly aware of hard, driving thrusts against his body, the convulsing and contracting heat.

There was only bliss. His orgasm melted his mind.

Marco's eyes fluttered open, settling on sated green eyes as the effects of his orgasm began to wane.

Christ, she's beautiful. Symone, her lips red and swollen, placed a soft kiss to the sensitive head of his cock as she stared up at him.

A shiver ran through him. He exhaled in short pants as he helped her to her feet. He held her weight while she trembled against him and Zander collapsed back onto the floor, his arms splayed out at his side.

Those dark eyes closed as his chest rose and fell rapidly. Christ, the man was hot. Marco's softening dick twitched and made an effort to fill. As he held Symone, he couldn't look away from Zander's strong, beautiful form, thick with ridged muscles, and hated that he'd agreed to the no-touching clause.

His mouth watered. He could practically taste the musky, male flavor on his tongue as he imagined licking his way across Zander's sweat-slicked chest. His hands itched to feel the strength in the sinew of his muscle. To explore beyond Zander's parted lips with his tongue. *One day*, he vowed.

He turned his attention back to the beauty in his arms and kissed her. Not with the same hungry, urgent need as earlier, but pure, slow seduction. He licked and nibbled at her lips, tasting himself.

"I taste good on you," he spoke against her lips, before diving into a full exploration of her mouth. He groaned at the mixture of the sweet and bitter of their combined flavors. He hungrily sought out every drop with his tongue. When he pulled back from the kiss, he licked the last bit of flavor from his lips. "I taste even better in you."

"I like you better in me too," Symone purred suggestively.

Marco shot a quick glance at Zander. "I think we broke him. Guess it's just you and me for round two."

"Not fucking likely," Zander protested as he rolled to his feet. He pressed a finger against Symone's hip, causing her to jerk. "I was simply admiring my marks on this sweet ass, trying to decide where to place the next one."

Symone shuddered against him as Zander ran that same fingertip up her spine.

"Anywhere you want, Z, as long as you stay out of my way. It's my turn to be buried in this luscious body."

Symone cocked her head to the side, studying him, her smile playful. "Well, Mr. Cantrell, the soft carpet is a great selling feature, but how sound is the furniture?"

In seconds, he had Symone flat on her back in the middle of his king-size bed. He covered her body with his and took her mouth in a searing kiss before the bed had even stopped bouncing.

"Sturdy enough for two, but the real test is how well it holds up to three," Zander challenged as he joined them on the bed. "More importantly, how accessible is it?"

Marco broke the kiss and looked at Zander, confused. "Accessible?"

Zander pushed a hand between them, pinching Symone's erect nipple, rolled it between his fingers. Symone gasped, and Zander took the opportunity to take his own kiss. "Uh huh," he replied into the kiss. "How handy are the amenities?"

What the fuck is he talking about? Accessible? Amenities?

Either Symone had sucked his brain out through his dick or Zander was babbling. "The what?"

"Condoms," they both responded with laughter.

Okay, so maybe a little of his brain was sucked out too, but damn, who could blame him? He reached over, opened the drawer and pulled out a thirty-six pack of Trojan Magnums, large size — thank you very much — and tossed them at a still laughing Zander. "Here are your fucking amenities."

Zander caught the box easily and studied it, before tossing them back at Marco and leering down at Symone. "That will get us started."

Marco ignored Zander's ambitious boast and spilled the contents of the box within reach. He lay on his side and traced a fingertip around Symone's nipple and down her belly until the muscles twitched. He leaned in and swiped the tip of his tongue across her erect nipple, eliciting a deep, satisfying moan from her. He smiled around the taut flesh. Zander's dark head lowered and he took her other nipple into his mouth.

"Oh God," she moaned under the dual assault.

Marco sucked hard using tongue and teeth to heighten her pleasure. He moved his hand down between her thighs. He closed his eyes at the feeling of her sex, wet and ready for him. He spread her wetness around her clit in slow circles. He teased her flesh, without actually touching where he knew she wanted it the most.

"Please... Mmm, more," Symone pleaded, her hips rising off the bed.

Zander's hand met his, moving lower, spreading her open while Marco slid his finger up and down her slit to settle back against her clit. While Zander teased her slit, Marco focused on her clitoris, alternated between soft and hard caresses. His cock twitched wildly.

She spread her legs wider, her hips rising toward their touch. Marco seized her leg and pulled it over his side, spreading her to him. He pulled off her swollen nipple and looked down to the sight of Zander's finger, glistening with Symone's juices, as it plunged in and out of her. He groaned, knowing it would soon be his cock moving in and out of her tight sheath.

"I-I need more... Harder," Symone begged as she thrashed between them.

Marco slid a finger in alongside Zander's. Symone arched her back, bucking wildly as she bore down on their fingers.

It was erotic as hell.

They worked in sync until her body was trembling. "That's it, baby, come for us," Zander encouraged, his voice thick with arousal.

Her answer was an incomprehensible cry as she threw her head back, body bowed tight, as her orgasm soaked their joined fingers.

She barely had time to recover from the strong orgasm they had pulled from her body with their talented fingers, before Marco was pulling her across his body.

Jesus, they were insatiable.

She drew in gasps of air as Marco positioned her just as he wanted her, his skin smooth against her inner thighs as she straddled him. She didn't know how much more pleasure she could take, heart hammering in her chest, her muscles melting. Could someone pass out from too much pleasure? She agonized over the thought for precious seconds before coming to the conclusion that she didn't care. She only knew that she wanted to find out just how much she could endure, consequences be damned.

"Fuck, Symone," Marco growled. "I have to have you."

With sure steady hands, he lifted her hips. As soon as the touch of his cock registered in her brain, he thrust up and impaled her on his long, thick cock. The sudden invasion tore a long pleasure-filled cry, from deep within her.

Zander and Marco surrounded her, filled her and completed her.

There was no longer any distinction between individuals, only a complete merging into one entity of ecstasy.

Chapter Fifteen

When you find the right one, everything changes.

His mother had been right, Marco thought as he lay in bed, Symone curled up at his side. Zander pressed tight against her back as his fingers drew lazy designs along the skin of her arm.

He wasn't sure what the change meant, only that something, a vital part of himself, had shifted in him since Symone had stepped through the door earlier. It was no longer merely a competition, a trophy for his shelf to collect dust, an object to look back upon with only memories of winning.

If asked, he couldn't tell if it was love beginning to sprout in his heart. He'd never cared for anyone beyond his family and the few friends he had. The only thing he was certain of at this moment was that he wanted to explore what was happening between them to the fullest. *Them* included Zander as well.

The man was sexy as fuck and brought his curiosity to a full-blown case of need to know. It wasn't just the lean muscular body or the dark exotic looks that he was attracted to. The man had an amazing mind. Just enough cocky swagger mixed in with intelligence, tenderness and humor. Everything about him sparked his interest. He wasn't sure what would happen between them, how far Zander would allow their relationship to evolve. But he knew he wanted him to be part of what was growing between him and Symone. He'd happily share her with him as his friend and hoped more would grow between the two of them later.

"You know, I really should be mad at the two of you," Symone grumbled, as she snuggled further against him.

"It was all his idea," Marco pled innocently.

"Sure it was." She swatted at him playfully. "Did mean, old Zander overpower you? Take over your home and bed, force you to do naughty, wicked things? Shame on you, Zander, for the corruption of this poor innocent man."

Zander huffed out an indignant grunt in response.

Marco ran the tip of his finger along her jawline, eliciting a shudder. "The naughty and wicked was all my idea."

Zander snorted and smiled. "Careful, I heard an overdose of bullshit can be hazardous to your health, Polo."

Symone chuckled and turned her head slightly toward Zander. "I just realized I don't even know your last name," she said to Zander with a small, embarrassed laugh.

Zander shot him a sharp look then settled his eyes back on Symone. "Ever...dt," he mumbled the last half.

Geez, what the hell had he done to deserve that nasty look? He hadn't asked for his name, though he was now more than a little curious. "What was that, Zoo-man?"

Zander's cheeks went pink. "Everhardt," he muttered.

Dead silence filled the room.

Marco's eyes went wide, giving Zander a disbelieving look. *You have to be fucking kidding me? Ever hard?*

Symone broke the silence. "I can attest to that," she giggled.

The color in Zander's face darkened.

"Ever hard," Marco snorted.

Zander stiffened and inhaled a sharp breath. "Everhardt," he corrected, drawing out the sound of the *d* and *t* at the end. Zander's eyes shifted back to his with a look of, 'give it your best shot, buddy' attitude.

Marco licked his dry lips. Hell yeah, he had noticed. Zander's cock wasn't as long as his but thicker. He'd witnessed how hard it was when he thrust in and out of Symone. Had seen how her lips had stretched wide to take his girth into her wet, hot mouth.

Oh, fuck yeah, I noticed.

The bulge in Zander's jeans, shorts, whatever he wore was like a magnet for his eyes. Symone wasn't the only one he was becoming addicted to. He met Zander's challenging eyes with a heated gaze. "I sure the hell noticed."

Zander just shook his head as if he knew there was no hope for him, but he didn't respond to the taunt. Instead, he looked at Symone. "What about you? Tell me something I don't know." Zander was learning Marco would give him that.

Symone nibbled at her bottom lip in concentration. "I'm not sure if there is much to tell. The two of you were pretty thorough in your interrogations. How about you just ask me something you want to know."

"Who broke your heart?" Zander asked.

Symone stiffened against him. He reached out and swatted Zander upside the head. Hard.

"Hey, what the fuck was that for?" Zander growled.

"That's not the kind of question you ask a woman when she's laying in your bed. Jesus, where the hell did you learn your social skills, Dickweed dot com?" Marco chastised.

Hell, he'd never had a steady girlfriend, had never wanted one, but even he knew enough not to bring up sensitive issues while lying naked in bed. Either things tended to get wet and messy with tears or sensitive, exposed parts got kneed.

"It's okay," Symone said softly. "I don't mind the question as long as you don't mind my right not to answer it."

Marco jumped in and spoke before the easy, comfortable feeling that was lingering around them was lost, "I'll tell you something neither of you know about me."

"Yeah, what's that," she prodded.

"Maggie called earlier in the week. I guess some fancy New York gallery wants to exhibit my paintings."

Symone threw her arms around his neck and screamed, the sound causing his ears to ring.

"Oh my God! I almost forgot to thank you. I mean that's so amazing about the gallery and you're going to do it right. Because…I mean… Wow! The painting you sent me was… I still can't come up with a word to describe it." She peppered his face with small, quick kisses. "Thank you. I wasn't going to keep it, but after tonight, I mean you know how could I not and…"

"Breathe, Symone," he chuckled. He pulled her onto his chest, cupping her face with both his hands forcing her to still. "Breathe, baby." He kissed the smile on her lips. "You're welcome."

Symone leaned into the kiss, begging for more, which he happily gave.

"That's great news, Polo. So when's the show?" Zander interrupted.

"Thanks, Z," he said sincerely when he came up for air.

He encouraged Symone to lay back down between them. She laid her head on his chest, the long strands of her hair tickling his skin. "The show is next month. It's not like they're doing a whole exhibit on me." He shrugged, grateful that the conversation had been diverted away from Zander's question but a little uncomfortable with the praise. "Just a couple pieces from some local artists, but Maggie seems pretty excited."

"As she should be," Symone praised. "You're an amazing artist. Which pieces are you going to send?"

He shrugged again. "I have some ideas but I'm sure Maggie will make the final choices. She knows this crap better than I do. I'm just the monkey behind the brush. Okay, enough of my shameless bragging, what about you, Z? What else haven't you told us about you?"

Zander resumed tracing his finger along the downy soft hair on Symone's arm.

What about him? Was there any interesting fact he could share? He seriously doubted they'd want to know anything about his childhood, not that there was really anything that interesting to tell.

Since entering the University of Florida when he was nineteen he'd been obsessed with his career. He made good money now and would probably be a multi-millionaire by the time he was thirty-five, but that sounded too much like bragging. Both Marco and Symone had seen his home, his car, knew what he did for a living, and bragging about the number of women he'd been able to seduce into his bed seemed an inappropriate topic. Since meeting them, he wasn't even really proud of that fact anymore, wasn't even certain that he ever had been. What else was there?

If he'd been asked a month ago if he was happy, he wouldn't have even hesitated before his affirmative answer. The rollercoaster ride of emotions since meeting Symone and Marco had made him think beyond his career goals. For the first time in his life, he realized just how lonely he truly was. He looked back at the two sets of expectant eyes watching him.

I bet you don't know that at this moment, I wouldn't give either one of you up.

It wasn't something he could share with them either, at least not right now. He couldn't think of a damn thing.

Zander fell back on what had always gotten him through uncomfortable questions in the past, his wit. He thrust his hips, shoving his hard shaft against Symone's ass. "I always live up to my name."

Symone threw her head back and yelped and he attacked her exposed neck. He sucked and bit at her tender flesh, effectively taking her mind off any more questions.

"Hold that thought, Z-Man," Marco encouraged as he leaped from the bed.

He raised his head to see Marco stroll out of the room. "Where the hell are you going?"

Marco stopped at the door, leaned against the doorframe, his impressive erection jutting proudly from the juncture of his thighs. He wasn't the only one that should be called *ever hard*. Marco was the perpetual horny bastard.

"I'm going to hide her purse and set the alarm." He turned, strode out of the room then called back, "I want more than sunshine touching my wood in the morning."

Symone's eyes went wide.

"Damn fine plan." He rolled Symone beneath him. *The fuck if I'm waiting, though.*

* * * *

Symone lay on her stomach in the middle of the large bed. Her dark hair and honey-colored skin stood in contrast against the stark white sheet. The top sheet draped across her lower body, exposing the creamy globe of one ass cheek and one long leg.

Zander lay on his side next to her, his body bereft of any covering. His right leg bent at the knee, denying Marco full access to all of Zander's delights. One hand rested at the middle of Symone's lower back. It was amazing how large his hand appeared against her lean form. His darker coloring was a sharp contrast to her lighter skin. With the early morning light streaming through the blinds, it gave the whole scene before him an otherworldly feel.

Marco leaned back in his chair and studied the sketch in his hand. He had captured the exotic masculinity of Zander, each ridge of muscle defined. Yet, with his eyes closed in slumber, he had also captured the softer side of the man.

Symone was the vision of sated seduction. Anyone viewing the sketch would be able to appreciate her beauty. The entire work was a study in sexuality, the powerful male with a possessive hand against his lover's back, the ravished beauty, sleeping peacefully and sated next to him.

The piece was some of his best work, and yet, he couldn't stop looking at the empty space on the other side of Symone. It felt incomplete. He looked back toward the bed and the space he had occupied earlier. He knew without a shred of doubt, he belonged there. For today, tomorrow, a year from now, he couldn't say. He only knew that he wanted to find out just where this unconventional union would go.

Symone shifted, drawing his eyes to her face. Sleepy green eyes blinked at him, a soft smile on her lips. "Hey," she whispered.

Marco closed his sketchbook, setting it and his pencils aside. "Morning," he said softly as he moved from the chair to kneel next to the bed. He pushed the dark strands of her hair back, fully exposing her gorgeous eyes. "How'd you sleep?"

"It started out pretty good, but didn't end so well."

His stomach clenched as if it had received a sharp jab. Was this where she was going to bail on them again? Avoid yet another morning-after scene with them? He had been hoping that the comfortable feeling that had settled over them the night before would still be there this morning.

Think of something to say, you big ox. His brain scrambled but came up empty.

She is gonna bolt if you just keep gawking at her with a stupid look on your face.

"I made coffee. Would that help?"

Smooth, Casanova, real smooth. He mentally gave himself a kick in the ass.

"No..."

In a blink of an eye, his brain ran down a mental list of things to say and he rejected all of them. He had never worried beyond one morning after before. His limited experience with it boiled down to another morning romp, a cup of coffee, sometimes breakfast, but beyond that, he was in new territory here.

"It's only the right side of my body that needs to be warmed up," Symone teased suggestively. She rolled to her back, exposing her full breasts, the dark pink nipples erect and begging for his attention.

A huge smile stretched across his face and his morning wood jumped for joy as Marco eased into the bed alongside her. Now this was territory he felt right at home in. He placed a kiss against an erect nipple.

Z-Man can come up with the witty shit to say later. It was his area of expertise, after all.

Marco pulled a tight nub into his mouth, sucking hard. Symone shuddered. This was his area of expertise.

Chapter Sixteen

With the scents of freshly brewed coffee and bacon filling the air, Symone sat at a small breakfast table, sipping coffee, dressed in nothing but her panties and one of Marco's very large T-shirts.

Marco stood at the stove, preparing breakfast in a pair of boxers. The muscles of his broad back and thick arms flexed, much to her delight, as he scrambled eggs in a pan. As she watched him move, a twinge of pain between her thighs reminded her just what a bad idea another round with the gorgeous man would be. The same reason why Zander was now showering alone.

She'd had to put her foot down, ignoring their pleas and pouts, and refuse to shower with them. They would take them alone or not at all because, dammit, she was too frickin' sore.

Keep their hands to themselves? Ha, they had no concept of personal space, and even as sore as she was, her stupid body was making a gallant effort to respond to them. Damn virile men. She turned away from

Marco's enticing body and scanned the large open-floor plan of the condo with a critical eye. It was a mix of eclectic and modern. Smooth, clean lines, neutral color palette with a few old-world wood pieces of furniture mixed in with the modern. It was masculine without being overly so. There were enough soft touches to compliment the strong. It was definitely a snapshot of its owner — a muscular construction worker who was also a tender artist.

"Your condo is very beautiful. Are you actually going to put it on the market or was it just part of your seduction plan?"

Marco looked over his shoulder. "Which answer will get me in the least amount of trouble?" he asked sheepishly.

She blew the steam from her coffee cup, before taking another small sip. Over the rim, she replied, "Neither, but your answer may be telling."

"In this economy — " He chuckled. He plated the eggs and bacon and brought two of them to the table, sitting one down in front of her. "I'd take one hell of a loss. That is if I could sell it at all."

"Mmm, good answer, sexy and smart." She glanced down at her breakfast. "And he cooks."

Marco set the other plate at an empty spot then brought a third plate over for himself and took a seat next to her. "Not just cook — " He took a large bite of egg. "I cook good."

She rolled her eyes at him, taking a small bite of her own eggs. "Good thing too, since you seem to be lacking in the modest department," she teased.

"Why be modest," he said around another huge bite of egg.

"And great table manners too I see."

"What? It's your fault. I usually have better manners but I'm starving." He winked and put another mouthful in. "I gotta keep up my strength if I'm going to keep up with a sex maniac like you."

Her coffee nearly ended up spewed across the table. That would teach her to laugh and drink at the same time.

"I can pick up your slack if you're not up to it," Zander said arrogantly as he strolled into the kitchen area and walked over to the coffee pot.

"Will you take care of us both then, big guy?"

"I'll take care of you all right," Zander replied as he brought his coffee to the table, and took the empty seat. He leaned over as if to give her a kiss.

She put her hands up to ward him off. "Don't you dare," she scolded. The disappointed expression on Zander's face almost had her backing down and allowing it. Then she shifted in her chair. *Ow! Nope, no kissing today, Symone.*

"I was just going to kiss you good morning," he said, a petulant look on his face.

"Yeah, tell that to the lower half of my body."

"Aw, someone is sore this morning," Marco razzed. He made a move to place his hand on her thigh.

She slapped it away.

Both of them laughed and despite her best efforts to be unaffected, the sound of their deep laughter and sexy faces made it hopeless. *Shower time.*

A very cold shower if she was smart. At least until the throbbing between her legs was under control, then she'd work on the other aching muscles.

She finished her now warm coffee in one gulp, set it down then stood. Pain shot up from her calf muscles. *Ouch.* Good God, it was going to be a long day. She jabbed a finger at both of them. "I swear if the two of you start high-fiving, I'm going to spank you both," she said with a wince.

The twin looks of lust on their faces had her groaning. *Kinky bastards.*

Turn away. If you say anything else, they will use it against us. Turn around and walk away. Save yourself. The little voice in her head was a bit dramatic, but the ache reminded her it was not that far off from reality. Gingerly, she turned and made her way toward the bathroom.

"Want some…?"

"No," she screamed in exasperation.

The sound of hands slapping, undoubtedly from the high-five they shared behind her back, resonated through the room.

I think I liked them better when they were competing against each other.

Once she had a shower, soothed certain parts, she'd give more thought to those spankings she owed them.

Ow! No thinking of spanking sexy asses either. Ow!

Zander watched Symone move slowly toward the bathroom. He tried not to laugh, but when Marco raised his hand for a high-five, how the hell was he supposed to turn down the opportunity of a little pat on the back posturing?

It wasn't that he didn't have any sympathy for Symone's pain. However, the male ego was pushing out front and center and demanding a little chest beating, or high-five as it was.

"So what's the next part of your plan?" Marco inquired.

He turned his attentions back toward Marco and started in on his breakfast. "What do you mean, next part of my plan?"

"Your plan to get Symone here was brilliant. Now what's the next move to keep her here?"

"I got her here, you figure out the next move." His lips curled into a sly grin. "I don't suggest using sex either. I think we pushed that one as far as we could." He snorted. "For the moment anyway."

Marco grinned and nodded. "From the way she was walking I'd say for longer than a moment."

Wait.

With the forkful of eggs midway to his mouth, Zander froze. He cocked his head at Marco. "No sex or walking?" he chuckled. "Damn glad I had the easy part of the plan. Good luck with that."

Marco frowned. "Uh... I believe you have just as much interest in this as I do."

Marco had a point there. He did have a big interest in this working out. Problem was he'd never had a relationship before and wasn't sure about the rules. If he admitted he was out of his element, would Marco use it against him? Take the advantage and run with it? They might have started out as competitors but he was pretty sure that somewhere in all of it, they'd started to become friends. At least he thought they had.

Fuck it, what have I got to lose?

"I'm not sure I'm going to be much help with this one," he said quietly. "I've never had a girlfriend before. The partying, seducing and fucking I got figured out, but after that, clueless," he admitted.

"No shit?" Marco asked, incredulous. He rolled his shoulders and shook his head. "Then we're fucked, because I haven't either."

Their eyes met and they both cracked up. What a fucking pair they were. The dumb leading the dumb.

"Flowers are a no-go," Zander snickered. "The girl at the florist shop is starting to creep me out."

"The blonde chick with the black nails and pink hoop in her nose?" Marco asked, still chuckling.

He nodded.

"Okay, I might have worn out my welcome there too."

Zander shook his head again and snorted. "No sex, no walking, you already fed her and no flowers. What the hell else do women want?"

"Beyond breakfast, I'm lost, Z."

They both finished their breakfast in silence. "So what do you think it is about Symone that has the two of us sitting here trying to figure out life's greatest mystery?" Zander asked seriously.

Marco set his fork down and drained his coffee. "I don't know if I can answer that, except to say, when she smiles or laughs it's like a drug. The more I see or hear it the more I want to be the one to make her smile and laugh. Every time I touch her or see her, I miss her a little more when she's gone." He looked thoughtful a moment. "I guess the only thing I can say for sure is she intrigues me. I want to know more about her."

"You really are an artist, aren't you?" he asked.

"Yeah, I guess." Marco shrugged. "What's that got to do with anything?"

"Because you are one sappy son of a bitch," he responded, wrinkling his nose in mock disgust.

"Fuck off," Marco replied, no real heat behind the words. "If you can explain it any better I'd love to hear your take on what makes her so irresistible." He leaned his elbows on the table and leered at him. "And don't give me any bullshit. You've got it just as bad as I do, or why else would you be willing to put up with my ass?"

Zander opened his mouth to make some flippant comeback then snapped his mouth shut. Sure, sometimes Marco annoyed the hell out of him, other times, fuck if he knew what it was he liked about him. He was willing to admit that he liked the guy... Sort of.

Hell, he'd even admit that the thought of sharing Symone with him just totally did it for him sexually. What he wasn't willing to admit, not to Symone, Marco, hell not even to himself, was that even Marco's innuendos gave him...

Stop right there. I'm not thinking about it, don't have any plans to think about it in the future, and damn sure am not finishing that thought.

"Fine," he admitted effectively, shoving aside further ideas about Marco and his stupid innuendos. "I got it bad. I'm still not going to babble on about smiles that are like drugs and whining like a lovesick puppy when she's gone." He stood and took his empty cup and plate to the sink. "So let me ask you, have you ever..." He turned back toward Marco, leaning against the counter. "Umm...you know, shared a woman before?"

"Sure I have, haven't you?" Marco said nonchalantly.

"Nope, gotta say this is all kinda new for me."

"Really?" he asked, eyebrow arching.

He didn't like the mischievous gleam in Marco's eye and he couldn't tell if he was fucking with him or was knocking him for not experiencing the male fantasy of two women in his bed, and technically he still hadn't. It had never been high on his priority list in the past and he had no idea how often the average Joe actually found himself in a ménage outside pornos and romance novels. This certainly had been his first. "So I'm not the first guy that's had to endure your bullshit."

Marco picked up his empty plate and moved to the sink, pushing him out of the way with a shoulder. His pulse sped. "Nope, you're the first guy lucky enough to experience the Marco Charm."

Marco charm? More like... He wasn't even sure what the hell it was Marco had, the fucker just confused the hell out of him most times.

Zander took a step to the side, moving farther from him, needing a little space from the man. He knew Marco was bullshitting him again but for some reason the tease made him feel uncomfortable. "Well, don't I just feel special," he said coolly. "You're so full of shit."

Marco finished rinsing his dishes and turned to lean back against the counter next to him. He crossed his broad arms over his chest. "Sometimes," he said with a smirk. "But you asked me if I'd shared a woman, not who I had shared her with."

Zander's stomach did a flip-flop, at the seductive tone in Marco's voice, a very unwanted reaction to the idea of being the first to share something with Marco. "You seem the type," he responded with a curt nod, ignoring the thrill that raced down his spine.

Marco's gaze wandered slowly down Zander's body and back up, looking directly into his eyes with a heated gaze. "Never had another man in my bed, though."

Zander thankfully controlled the urge to squirm under Marco's appraisal, scolding himself once again for his reaction to Marco. He narrowed his eyes at him, standing ramrod straight. "Why the fuck do you always talk like that? I swear if I didn't know any better..."

Symone cut off the rest of his statement as she walked back into the room. "Anyone up to cocktails and lazing around on the beach?" she asked as she toweled her wet hair.

Both he and Marco stared at each other. Zander glared, but Marco's look was playful, though the challenge was still evident.

Zander forced himself to turn away from the challenge. "I'm up for anything you are today." He moved toward her.

"Sounds like a plan to me," Marco agreed. "Just let me grab a shower and I'll be ready." He strolled by on his way to the shower, and son of a bitch if Zander didn't notice the tent in Marco's boxers.

The arrogant bastard wasn't just teasing. And for fuck sakes why am I hard!

The thought made him slightly ill. He grabbed Symone, wrapped his arms around her. He needed that morning kiss. Bad!

Chapter Seventeen

The sound of the doorbell caused Symone's stomach to react as if a thousand butterflies had suddenly taken flight.

It wasn't like it was unexpected, hell she'd invited Zander and had been expecting him. The thing was, other than the first time she'd met him at Posey's for lunch, she hadn't spent any alone time with him.

Yes, it had been a stupid attempt at trying to keep from seeing him as a real person instead of just a sexual object but in her defense, at the time it had seemed like a damn good plan. Funny how sometimes the best-laid plans have a way of changing. Or, in this case, evolved into something she hadn't thought she wanted.

Truth be told, even her earlier declaration that she'd just follow along, see where things would go, had turned out to be a load of crap. The past week had proven it.

Zander had been out of town wooing a major client, Marco had been swamped at work—when he wasn't

SJD Peterson

working, he was preparing for the upcoming art exhibition—while she had sat home, completely miserable, missing them both terribly.

When Zander had called earlier this morning saying he was coming back into town this afternoon and wanted to see her, she hadn't even hesitated to say yes. She had immediately called Marco, squealing like an adolescent girl and excitedly informed him that Zander was coming back and asked him to join them.

She hadn't asked him to come because she was afraid to be alone with Zander, but because...well because they just all kind of belonged together. She was sure Marco felt the same way, and even though he couldn't get away from work, he did plan on meeting them for dinner later.

The weirdest thing was, he hadn't sounded the least bit jealous and in fact had given her the impression that he was just as excited as she was about the three of them getting together later.

The soft knock snapped her out of her musings. Smoothing down her hair, she walked over and opened the door. Symone felt as if her heart stopped dead in her chest and her breath whooshed out of her lungs.

Zander stood on the other side of her door dressed in a dark charcoal-gray Armani suit, tailored perfectly to his powerful body, roses in hand and the sexiest smile she'd ever seen in her life. She couldn't speak or move, hell she couldn't even breathe, he had affected her so deeply and so completely.

Then she didn't have to try to think of anything other than Zander's arms around her as he grabbed her and took her mouth in a deep, claiming kiss that flat-out curled her toes and soaked her panties.

Zander pulled her closer as he broke the kiss, speaking against her temple. "Christ, I missed you." Soft kisses to her temple, forehead and cheek accentuated each word.

Symone clung to him, holding on to his strength as she melted into his touch. "I missed you too," she admitted. It shocked her how much she'd missed him, but she had.

When he swept her up into his arms, dropping the roses on the entryway table, she expected him to carry her to the bedroom. Her body rejoiced, the walls of her sex wept and her skin electrified in anticipation. But to her utter amazement he took a seat on the couch and situated her on his lap, one arm securely around her back as if he were cradling her. With a fingertip from his free hand, he stroked her cheek. "How was your morning?"

Tears prickled at the back of her eyes at the tenderness in his voice. They had talked on the phone nearly every night since he'd been gone, but the simple act of asking her about her morning instead of whisking her off to the bedroom tugged at her heart. It spoke volumes that it wasn't about the sex, well not *just* about the sex because that was amazing, but he felt more.

"It was fine," she finally answered, her voice breaking a little with emotion. "How was your flight?"

He placed his hand on her hip, rubbing and caressing her. "Better than the flight out. This time I was looking forward to what was waiting for me on the other end."

Dammit, there he went again, making her eyes burn with tears and her chest constrict. When he looked at her with soft brown eyes and said things like that, he made it impossible to control her emotions.

Yes, she was coming to terms with it, the wall sliding down slowly, but that didn't mean it still didn't scare the hell out of her. It also didn't mean she was ready to let the wall completely crumble.

"I called and told Marco you were coming in today. He wants to meet us for dinner."

"Yeah, I know."

There was no trace of jealousy that she'd called Marco and told him he was coming, he just accepted it. She arched an eyebrow at him. "How do you know I called Marco?"

"He called me," Zander replied with a nonchalant shrug.

"He called you?"

"Uh huh, wanted to know where I wanted to eat dinner." He kissed the tip of her nose and smiled. "He said you were a little excited to see me and hung up before the two of you could make plans."

Wait! Aren't they supposed to be competitors?

It wasn't like she hadn't noticed how much friendlier they had become but she hadn't realized that they had spoken since they had worked together to lure her to Marco's condo.

"Did you two flip a coin again?" she asked. Maybe she was reading too much into this.

"Nah. I told him I was sick of eating in restaurants so he's making us dinner."

Nope, she hadn't read too much into it. Marco was offering to make them dinner and he hadn't been jealous or freaked out that she was going to be spending a couple hours alone with Zander. When the hell had she missed this new twist?

"Wait a minute... Marco is cooking us dinner. Not me, but *us*?" She was completely confused.

Zander chuckled at what was surely a befuddled look on her face and kissed her cheek. "Yes, *us*. As in, you, me and Marco."

"What… Wait…what did I miss?"

He wasn't making any sense. Yes, she had hoped they could all spend time together and get to know each other. She never wanted to have to make a choice between them, but she also never imagined that it would be easy or that they would agree to it so quickly.

"What's not to understand?" Zander asked as he slid his fingers beneath the hem of her dress, his large hands kneading and massaging the muscles of her thigh, setting off sparks of arousal to race across her skin. "We both want you." He leaned in and mouthed against her neck. "Neither of us is willing to back away."

Symone leaned her head back and gave him more room to work, moaning as he nipped and licked at her neck.

"You don't want us to, do you, Symone?" he whispered in a gravelly voice.

Hell no she didn't want them to back away but damn.

"How…" She wanted to ask him how and why they had come to this agreement, but the words morphed into a moan as his hand inched further up her leg and his tongue traced the shell of her ear.

"Easy," he said confidently. "You want him." He moved his hand to her panties, one finger teasing at the silk fabric. "You want me."

Symone gasped as that exploring finger brushed gently against her slit, her body instinctively moving closer, pushing into his touch. "I do," she confessed.

"We want to give you exactly what you want."

Symone had no doubt in her mind that she wanted him — the pulse throbbing between her thighs made it pretty evident just how badly. She was also convinced beyond a shadow of a doubt that Zander wanted her, as was evident in the hard shaft pressed against her ass. But his statement made her stomach clench, and not the good kind of feeling either.

God, she was a mess. One minute she didn't want anything from them but meaningless, mind-blowing sex and now the thought of them doing something they normally wouldn't do just to please her sexually hurt her heart.

Christ, you're a crazy bitch. He's offering you exactly what you wanted, why do you care why he's offering it?

The thought hit her so hard and so deep that it felt as if her soul was being ripped to pieces. She hated that voice in her head, hated even more that she had created that persona. She had become the person she had despised for hurting her in the past, no better than Kyle or Greg, or even Travis. She had used her body instead of her heart to get what she wanted, and in turn, caused these two men to accept something they never would have otherwise.

She sat upright, pushing his hand away and scurried off his lap. Her breath came in painful gasps and her mouth filled with saliva as she fought to keep from being sick. She was more ashamed of herself than she could ever remember being and she turned away, not able to look Zander in the eye.

Strong arms wrapped around her. Zander pulled her tight against his chest and made "shhh" sounds against her ear. The hold she'd been trying to keep on her emotions since the moment she'd left her house weeks ago and stepped into Menjo's came pouring out of her in a rush of tears. Powerless against the storm, she started to shake from the intensity of the sobs ripped straight from her heart.

Zander picked her up into his arms, turned her to cradle her head against his chest, and she buried her face against him hiding. His tenderness and soft-spoken words of comfort as he carried her to the couch and held her should have eased the outburst, but instead they intensified it. She didn't deserve his kindness, hadn't earned it, and the worst part of it all was that she was still a selfish bitch. She felt bad for what she had done to them but the majority of her tears were for herself, her own shame.

And yet, she let him hold her as he rubbed her back and stroked her hair, accepting his comfort until she cried herself to sleep.

Panic.

Dry mouth, quivering muscles, sick roll of his stomach — it was definitely panic.

Zander had no fucking clue what had just happened, what he had said or done to make Symone cry.

One minute he'd been kissing and teasing, the next comforting and trying to soothe away her tears. He must have said something wrong, done something because why else would she now be lying in his arms having just cried herself to sleep?

Looking down at her sleeping form, his mind raced a mile a minute and he just couldn't get it. "What the hell did I do?" he whispered. He pushed back the hair from her face and gently wiped away the tears still lingering on her cheek. His chest tightened at the sight, and in that moment, he would do anything to make her smile again.

He had no experience with crying females, hadn't ever had a morning-after before Symone. This was way out of his realm of expertise and in a moment of clarity, as the adrenaline surging through his system began to calm, he knew exactly what he had to do. He carefully reached into his suit jacket, pulled out his cell and hit speed dial. He needed reinforcements and fast.

The instant the phone stopped ringing, he spoke before he even heard a hello. "Get your ass over here now!" he whispered.

"What... Z-Man, is that you? Speak up, dude."

"I said get your ass over to Symone's now," he growled low.

"What the hell is going on? I'm just leaving the site and still have to stop at the store..."

Zander didn't give a fuck about the site or stores. Goddammit, he needed the man to be here ten minutes ago. He interrupted Marco's babbling, "She started crying and I have no idea what the hell to do."

Silence.

"Did you hear me?" Zander whispered a little louder. He didn't want her to wake up before Marco had a chance to get there because sure as shit he would either do or say something to make it worse.

"You made her cry?" Marco's tone was like ice. "I'm on my way."

The phone went dead and Zander sighed in relief.

He could deal with Marco's anger. It didn't worry him in the slightest. What he couldn't deal with was seeing Symone's tears when she woke up. It had broken his heart and he hated how powerless he'd felt. If he had any doubts before, he sure as hell knew exactly how he felt now. He would do anything to make her happy and never cause another tear to fall from her eyes.

He was falling completely head over heels in love with her.

* * * *

When Symone woke up, she was lying in Zander's arms with her face against his chest. His suit was damp from her tears, and he was rubbing her back and speaking in hushed tones with someone. She looked to the other end of the couch and saw Marco and warmth filled her chest at seeing him. A second later, the sickening feeling of ice rushed through her veins as her shame came back full force causing her to whimper.

"Hey, you're awake," Marco said softly.

Symone gave him a small smile and looked up to meet Zander's concerned eyes. He placed a small kiss to her forehead and squeezed her briefly. "I'm sorry I made you cry," he said sincerely.

Symone looked away but moved up and buried her head in his neck. She shook her head and against his skin, adamantly said, "I'm so sorry."

She sensed Marco moving from his spot on the couch and she was suddenly wrapped in both of their warmth as he pressed up against her side and nuzzled her neck. The three of them sat there. No one spoke, just held on to each other.

When she finally got what she wanted—needed—to say straight in her mind, she lifted her head and kissed Zander softly on the lips first, then Marco. She cleared her throat. "I made myself cry. I've been so stupid and selfish."

"Symone," Zander started to speak, but she stopped him with another small kiss.

"Please, just let me get this out before I lose my nerve."

They nodded and remained silent as they continued to caress and rub her legs and back.

"I've been trying so hard to be someone I'm not. This carefree, non-emotional seductress just isn't me. I realized today that I've become just like the people who hurt me in the past. I used you both and I'm so very sorry. I can't do this anymore. I thought..." Symone stared down at her hands as she wrung them tightly together. "I thought I could finally let go and be me again, the real me and let my true emotions finally come out from behind this wall I had built. To let you both know how much I care about you."

Symone had to stop and take a few deep breaths, her chest squeezing painfully tight. She had to get this out, all of it. She swallowed, forcing down the lump that had formed in her throat then continued, "Then, Zander, you said you two would give me anything I wanted and it was at that moment when I realized what my selfishness had cost you both. What it made the two of you do, and I'm so very sorry." She wiped angrily at the tears that slid down her cheek. She didn't want or deserve their sympathy.

"Hey, wait a minute," Marco said, pulling her into his arms tighter, "come here, it's my turn to hold you."

She shifted into his arms, wanting to feel them wrapped around her at least one more time. His warmth instantly engulfed her and her heart cracked even further with the knowledge of what she was losing.

Marco didn't give her the option of hiding her face. He tipped her head back with one hand as he held her tight with the other. "You have nothing to be sorry for and you didn't *make* us do anything we didn't want to do. Do you think when I first spotted you in Menjo's that I thought to myself, man that's a great lady, I wonder what kind of girlfriend or wife she would make." He looked at her with a serious but tender expression on his face.

"No," she admitted.

"You're right, the moment I laid eyes on you, the first thing I thought was, damn I want some of that. When I saw you dancing with Zander the game was on. I didn't think about your feelings, or his or anything else other than how soon I could get you out back and fuck you against the wall." He chuckled.

Zander swatted at Marco's head, laughing as he moved up closer and snuggled up to her. "Way to sweet talk, you Neanderthal."

Marco arched an eyebrow at Zander. "You were thinking the same thing so shut up."

"You're right, but damn you could use a little tact — you know, couth?"

Symone couldn't help but laugh at their antics and the tightening in her chest began to ease.

"Yeah, whatever." Marco rolled his eyes at Zander and turned back to her. "I liked spending time with you, sketching you, looking at you." He waggled his brows. "But even after the first night we all spent fu... I mean screwing around, I still didn't think too much about your feelings, only about nailing you again. Hell, Symone, that's a new thing for me, I haven't ever even had a second date before you, and neither has Z-Man."

"Okay, Polo, you're done. Just sit there and look cute. Let me take over here before you make her cry again. This time from laughing at your crude ass." He tried pulling her back over onto his lap but Marco refused to let go.

"I'm saving you here, it's kind of hard to think of the right thing to say when she's sitting on your... Well, you know what it's like." Marco shrugged. "Sorry, Symone."

She was starting to understand what it was Marco was getting at and as it sunk in the tightness in her chest eased completely and her stomach no longer felt like it was trying to decide if the small lunch she'd had was worth the effort of expelling it. "It's okay," she said, wiggling her hips playfully and laughing when Marco groaned.

"Behave," Zander scolded them. "What caveman here is trying to say is you didn't make us do anything we didn't want to do. We knew the game and the score. We've both been playing at it a long time." He lifted her chin and looked directly into her eyes. "You, my dear, suck at the game."

"Mmm, I can attest to that," Marco purred and nuzzled her neck.

Zander jabbed a finger at him. "You're not helping." He looked back at her. "Here's the thing, Symone. Nobody ever sees someone across a room for the first time or meets a stranger and thinks anything beyond the physical. It's only when they pass the physical checklist that we make our move. Every relationship, whether it lasts a night, week or a lifetime starts out the same way. For the first time in my life, I looked at something past the physical and even though you were trying to hide her, I saw you and I liked what I saw. I want to know everything about you, and who knows how long it will last, but I know I want to find out. I want to learn why my chest hurts when you leave, why I can't think about anything except you when you're gone and how your smile instantly puts one on my face. Honestly" — he leaned in and spoke that last words of his sentence against her ear — "I think you can make my life worthwhile."

"You son of a bitch," Marco growled at Zander. "You got that from me, you stole my damn line."

"I know, I learned from the master sap," Zander chuckled and gave him a proud smile. "It's still true."

Symone couldn't help but giggle at the pout on Marco's face. He was always the tender one and said the sweetest things, while Zander tended to use his wit to make her smile. She knew Marco was telling the truth, which meant that Marco had told Zander how he felt, but why? She understood the physical attraction was the first feeling and was relieved that she had been so transparent to them but it still didn't explain why they were willing to put up with each other. Or were they? Was it going to come down to a choice eventually? Would she have to make a choice between them and if it did how could she? *I can't.*

She ran the back of her hand lightly down Zander's check, staring into his deep brown eyes. "I get it, it's just that…" She waved her hand between them, unsure how to ask the question.

Marco took her hand in both of his. "I got this one," he said, clearly speaking to Zander but looking straight at her. "Z-Man told me what all he had said before you started to cry and trust me on this, we both want you, and what's wrong with giving you what you want?"

"But the competition…"

"No buts," Marco interrupted. "We're not doing anything we don't want to do. Sure we started out trying to outdo one another. One hell of a thrill to best a top dog, I won't deny that, but somewhere along the way it stopped being about knocking him down or winning anymore. I started to like the irritating bastard, kinda like having him around."

"Yeah, I love you too," Zander chaffed. "You're still not getting my ass."

"Want to flip a coin for it?" Marco countered.

The look of panic on Zander's face had her and Marco laughing. Poor Zander, he was trying but he couldn't hold back his own laughter.

"So what do you say, Symone? Ready to see where this unorthodox, unconventional and totally crazy ride takes us?" Marco asked still chuckling.

That was the million-dollar question, wasn't it. She'd run the full spectrum of emotions today but it still came down to one simple choice.

Was she ready to accept what they were offering and hope like hell that things worked out? Or was she going to be a coward and miss the dance?

Chapter Eighteen

Warm water soothed her aching muscles and the scents of Egyptian musk, precious amber and vanilla bourbon eased Symone's mind as she soaked in a bath infused with Carol's Daughter of Ecstasy.

Linda's Daughter of Ecstasy would be a better name because this daughter was totally feeling it.

It would be perfect except that chatting with a pouting Sedesa on the phone wasn't really conducive to the whole relaxing thing.

"I called you in plenty of time this morning and you said you were up and packed. How did you miss your flight?"

"I was up and packed," Sedesa defended. "It was all Ian's fault."

"Uh-huh."

Sedesa wasn't the type of person to let schedules or deadlines worry her. More of a free spirit who floated around on a wind that was always ten minutes slow.

"It was his fault this time, honest. I bent over to pick up my carry-on bag, wanted to make sure I had everything, you know?"

"And you were missing something and this is Ian's fault how?" Symone asked, confused.

"Well... I didn't actually get a chance to check the bag, because when I bent over I heard a loud groan and the next minute I was naked, thrown on the bed and Ian..."

"Stop right there," Symone interrupted, laughing. "I got the picture, I don't need the fine details. Were you able to get another flight?"

"Yeah, we're at the airport. I had to use my girlish charm but I managed to get on a flight and we should make it just in time. Though I doubt we'll make it for cocktails."

Symone's skin prickled with the sensation that someone was watching her. She looked toward the door and found a very sexy Zander leaning against the doorframe staring at her, wearing a white robe. As her eyes roamed from his gorgeous face downward, her pulse increased. He wasn't just sexy. He was a very sexy, very horny Zander as evident by his large cock pressing out against his robe.

"See you when you get here." She hit the 'Off' button and tossed the phone to the floor. Zander's presence so overwhelmed her that it was hard to form words. "Hey," was the only thing she could squeeze past her constricted throat.

"Hey, yourself," he replied in a husky voice as he stepped further into the bathroom. "Who was that on the phone?"

"Phone?" Who cared who was on the phone? She'd been reduced to simple replies of one syllable words and even those were becoming more difficult as he moved closer still.

"Yes, Symone, who are you going to see when they get here?" He went to his knees next to the tub and ran a fingertip from her neck down her breastbone. A shudder went through her.

"Or, better yet, how long do we have before they get here?" His tone was deep, the desire unquestionable in his tone and heavy-lidded dark eyes.

Symone's chest tightened as she looked up at him. She had spent so much time trying to keep him at arm's-length, had been so afraid of what if's, that she had nearly missed out on having this amazing man in her life. Christ, she was a lucky woman.

"Sedesa." She reached up and ran her fingers through his thick hair, fisted it and tugged him closer. "We have plenty of time," she whispered against his lips.

A low groan rose up from deep in his chest. She felt it all the way to her core. His mouth covered hers, his tongue demanding entrance.

"Symone."

He sighed into the kiss as she parted her lips, pushed his tongue deeper into her, exploring and devouring her mouth. She whimpered and clutched the back of his head, pulling him closer to her, sucking on his tongue as it darted in and out of her mouth.

Zander broke the kiss and slid his arms around her. He pulled her from the tub and wrapped her in his robe. "Hang onto my neck," he encouraged as he stepped out of the bathroom and moved toward the bed, drying her with his robe, hands exploring and rubbing every part of her body he could reach. As soon as they made it to the bed, he placed her on top and covered her with his heat. He kissed her again, hard and fierce.

His body against hers, the hard planes of his body and thick cock pressed to her stomach. The walls of her sex contracted in anticipation of feeling him deep inside her. "Want you," she pleaded into the kiss.

His breath came out in short puffs and his gaze bore into hers. "I'm all yours. Want you to ride me, babe. Take what you want, what we both need." Zander's hand moved down her body, a gentle glide, urging her to move with him as he rolled onto his back. "I can't wait to be inside you. Get me ready for you," he begged in between soft kisses and licks to her lips.

Symone moaned at his naughty words, and the feel of his throbbing shaft against her poured liquid fire through her veins. She placed one last kiss to his lips and reluctantly rolled away. Grabbing the sweet almond oil and a condom from the bedside table, she hurriedly moved back to kneel next to him, his hard cock jutting up proudly from his body made her mouth water. Symone bent down, and with the tip of her tongue, licked the small pearl of pre-cum glistening from his slit, moaning in appreciation as his flavor exploded across her tongue.

"Fuck." Zander hissed at the contact. "Don't tease me, babe, won't last. Need you so much."

Her breath caught as her oil-covered fingers stroked his cock. He was so hard he had to be aching. She didn't tease. Her own need caused her head to spin, and she made quick work of rolling on the condom, covering his sheathed cock in more oil as he trembled beneath her.

Not wanting to wait another second to feel him deep inside her, she moved to straddle his lap but he stopped her. He moved down to the edge of the bed until his feet touched the floor and leaned back on his elbows. "Turn around. I want to watch in the mirror as you take my cock."

The large mirror on the dresser was at the perfect height and position. Jesus, he drove her insane with lust. She would never tire of his naughty mind and wicked body.

Each moment with him made her crave him even more. She couldn't ever get enough of him in or out of bed. She took one last kiss and moved into position as he'd asked. Grasping his cock in her hand, she straddled him, moving forward until the head of his cock pressed against her wet slit. Symone lifted her gaze and met his in the mirror.

Time stopped and she hovered above him, body trembling with need, and heart so full, she thought it might burst from the look in his dark eyes. "I'm yours," she whispered and took him into her body in one quick movement. She pressed her ass against his tight stomach.

Zander cried out and heat spiraled through her body. She shuddered with the force of the need he ignited in her. Holding his dark eyes with hers, she began to move, rolling her hips in small circles, then moved up until just the head of his cock was still held inside her before plunging back down to the hilt.

As their bodies moved perfectly together, closer and closer to release, Zander encouraged her to lean back against him and rest her head against his shoulder. He started to thrust into her with strong snaps of his hips. "God, you feel so good. Love the way you feel around me."

Symone squeezed her eyes closed, breath coming in shallow pants as she fought to hold on, not wanting the moment to end.

* * * *

Marco walked into the hotel room and his breath rushed out of him. His dick went instantly hard at the sight before him.

Symone straddled Zander on the bed, her back to his chest and head against his shoulder. The most beautiful look of pleasure he'd ever seen on her face.

Fuck, I'm a lucky son of a bitch.

All thoughts of art exhibits and everything else fled his mind, his sole focus on joining the two people who had become his whole world over the last few weeks.

His shaft went from hard to aching. Zander tracked him with his eyes as he thrust up hard into Symone. Marco pulled and ripped at his clothes as he moved further into the room.

Completely naked by the time he reached the bed, he dropped to his knees between Zander's spread legs. The muscles in Zander's legs trembled as Marco ran his hands up his muscular thighs, the soft hair tickling his palms.

Momentarily speechless, he sat enthralled as he watched Zander's thick shaft, wet and glistening with Symone's juices as he pistoned in and out of her tight slit. He needed to taste her. Wrapping a fist around his own throbbing dick, he pulled hard, leaned in and licked Symone from clit up to her navel with the flat of his tongue. He sucked and nibbled at her skin until he felt her hand in his hair and he looked up to meet her stunning green eyes.

"There's what *we* were missing," Symone panted as she stroked his cheek.

Marco moved up and took her mouth in a blistering kiss. He plunged his tongue deep and claimed her as thoroughly as she did him. Symone wrapped her hand around Marco's, and together they stroked him, pulling a deep moan from him. Breaking the kiss, he panted into her mouth, breathing each other in for a moment.

"What about the show?" she asked softly.

"Mags has it under control. We have an hour before we have to be down in the lobby."

"Good," Zander bit out past clenched teeth, hips snapping. "Because I'm kind of busy here and you're blocking my view."

Marco and Symone both laughed. Symone's laughter turned into a whimper as Zander started to thrust in earnest.

"Impatient bastard," Marco grumbled easily as he licked his way back down Symone's body.

"Uh huh, you try to be patient from where I'm sitting, lying…whatever."

Symone shut Zander up and reduced him to incoherent babbling as she began to meet each one of his thrust with a hard one of her own. Marco returned to his position on his knees and licked, sucked and nibbled on Symone's clit and all talking ceased. Moans, pleas and whimpers filled the air around them.

When he eased a finger in alongside Zander's cock, Symone arched her back "Oh yes, that's it. More, faster."

Marco loved the way the hard steel of Zander's shaft and Symone's tight channel felt against his flesh. A perfect combination of hard and soft, and he had to taste them, all three of them. He licked down, tongue swirling around Symone's entrance, lapping her juices from the base of Zander's cock and his own plunging finger.

With his other hand he continued to pull hard on his cock, his hips snapping to meet their rhythm. Their cries filled the air and the frenzy increased, pushing them closer and closer to release.

Symone's orgasm was like a match to a wick. Their names on her lips and the tight contractions of her sex clamping down on him and Zander detonated an explosion. Zander thrust one last time deep inside Symone, his shouts echoing hers. It ripped the last thread of restraint Marco had, and with one last hard stroke, he was shooting his pleasure on the bed skirt and Zander's thighs.

Marco lazily lapped and kissed the skin of Symone's right hip and petted the thick muscles of Zander's thigh as they tried to slow their breathing and waited for the trembling to calm. The familiar sounds and scents surrounding him eased him and he knew he was exactly where he was supposed to be.

Yeah, he was one lucky son of a bitch all right.

Epilogue

*"If you're able to be yourself, then you have no competition.
All you have to do is get closer and closer to that essence."*
~ *Barbara Cook*

Standing in a room full of people at a black-tie gala was not one of the top ten events Marco hoped to experience in his lifetime. The sensation of being choked by the unfamiliar bow tie, the snooty air of many in attendance and the sick feeling in the pit of his gut at being the center of their attention made the event one of those life experiences he'd preferably never have to live through. Kind of like a root canal.

Standing at the podium, he shifted uncomfortably from foot to foot, searching the crowd until his eyes settled on the faces of those important to him and some of the tension eased. Maggie's huge smile reminded him of the way his mom used to look at him when making a big deal out of even the smallest of his accomplishments. Since meeting him, she had become the biggest fan of his work since his mom had died.

Even the smiles of his new friends, Sedesa and Ian, helped relax him, but the pride in Symone's and Zander's gazes affected him the deepest. He felt their smiles deep in his soul. Those smiles had become what he yearned to see the most, each and every day.

Taking one last deep breath, and drawing strength from his friends and lovers, he addressed the crowd.

"Mr. S. Miarka and the staff of RC Gallery, ladies and gentlemen, and my friends, a very good evening to you all. I am pleased and honored to display my work here at RC Gallery. Thank you for your kind words for the pieces already on display. Umm..."

Okay, this was worse than he'd thought it was going to be. Every eye in the crowd seemed to bore into him and made his skin crawl. His heartbeat increased to an uncomfortable level and he realized that being the sole focus of anyone other than Symone and Zander just wasn't something he figured he'd ever be comfortable with.

The rest of the speech and the questions about the subject matter and technique that followed were a blur. The praises for his depiction of Symone as well as the painting he'd done of the two of them on the beach were a huge hit. Still, the only thing he could think of was how quickly the three of them could return to Wakulla and start living their lives together.

Marco graciously thanked everyone for coming and their questions. When the room grew silent, he reached for the cord that would reveal his hidden painting.

"This piece I call *The Essence of the Challenge*." He tugged the cord, revealing the painting beneath.

Symone was thankful for Zander's strong arm around her waist to steady her when the black velvet curtain fell to the ground.

A collective gasp resounded through the room then the crowd erupted in applause. Symone clung to Zander as tears seeped from her eyes. She remembered the scene well. It was the first morning she'd woken up in their arms, the first time she'd stopped running. Marco had painted them in awe-inspiring realism.

On her stomach, a white sheet covering part of her lower body, and Zander at her left side, one arm raised above his head.

What stole her breath was that Marco had painted himself to her right, one arm also stretched above his head, the other hand entwined with Zander's against her lower back.

The applause began to fade, and Symone watched with her heart in her throat as Marco made his way to them. He stopped a few feet from them, his smile shy. "What do you two think?" he asked clearly uncertain.

Zander pulled Marco closer, slapped him on the back, before they both wrapped their arms around him. Symone looked up and begged a kiss, which Marco gave tenderly without hesitation.

"It's absolutely stunning. I'm so proud of you," Symone said.

"Yeah me too," Zander agreed. "I see what you've been going on and on about. I do have a great ass, don't I?"

Marco rolled his eyes, and they all laughed, before Marco's expression turned serious. "I had great inspiration. Thank you both." His voice broke as he tried to hold back the well of emotions. He was thanking them for something much deeper than posing for the painting.

His eyes, though, told her everything he was feeling. His beautiful hazel eyes were full of sincerity and happiness, and an abundant amount of love made his eyes sparkle and her heart rejoice. They held on to each other for long moments, letting their happiness surround them.

Zander finally broke the silence. "Go thank the rest of your adoring fans. I think Maggie is going to explode if she doesn't get a hug soon," he teased, nodding toward Maggie who stood behind them vibrating. His voice lowered in a husky whisper only loud enough for the three of them to hear. "The sooner you thank everyone, the sooner the three of us can celebrate your success properly."

Marco was more than ready to shed the monkey suit and spend his night, all night and the rest of his life, celebrating with Zander and Symone. He placed one last kiss to Symone's lips, squeezed Zander's shoulder and stepped back. "Don't either of you move, this will be the shortest after-party reception for a guest they have ever witnessed here at RC Galleries."

Before he could turn away, Zander's voice stopped him. "Hey, Marco?"

He felt tears burn at the back of his eyes at Zander's simple act of using his real name for the first time. "Yeah?"

"Here ya go." He held out his hand, a coin sitting in his palm. "I don't need lady luck anymore, I got everything I need." Zander waited until he took the coin before he and Symone moved toward the refreshment table.

Marco stared at the coin, head up and flipped it over and started to chuckle. "Son of a bitch," he muttered as he revealed the other head imprinted into the opposite side of the coin.

"Hey, Zander," he yelled out. He waited until Zander turned his head and met his gaze. "Thanks for the luck. Your ass is so mine!"

He turned, laughing boisterously at the panicked look on Zander's face, then went to give Maggie a hug.

About the Author

SJD Peterson, better known as Jo, hails from Michigan. Not the best place to live for someone who hates the cold and snow. When not reading or writing, Jo can be found close to the heater, checking out NHL stats and watching the Red Wings kick a little butt. Can't cook, misses the clothes hamper nine out of ten tries, but is handy with power tools.

SJD loves to hear from readers. You can her contact information, website details and author profile page at http://www.pride-publishing.com.